LACY FROM LARAMIE

NORA NOLAN

Published by Blushing Books
An Imprint of
ABCD Graphics and Design, Inc.
A Virginia Corporation
977 Seminole Trail #233
Charlottesville, VA 22901

Nora Nolan
Lacy from Laramie

eBook ISBN: 978-1-64563-896-4
Print ISBN: 978-1-64563-897-1
v2

PROLOGUE

Laramie, Wyoming Territory, mid 1880's

"You look beautiful, Lacy. I daresay no bride ever looked more so," Amelia Hardy said to her daughter as she adjusted her veil. She kissed Lacy's forehead just before she lowered the sheer fabric.

"Thank you, Mother." There was no joy in her voice, only resignation.

"Oh, Lacy, you might as well accept it. We're just lucky Carl stepped up and agreed to marry you. You would have been ruined."

"But I wasn't ruined, Mother. Carl didn't compromise me at all. It isn't fair and you know it."

Amelia sat down and sighed. "Fair has nothing to do with it and *you* know it. You two were out all night and he didn't bring you home until morning. Perhaps it might have been different if we hadn't had guests, but you know how people are. We didn't have any choice but to insist that he protect your reputation."

"My reputation was spotless. So is Carl's. He's a good man, an honorable one, or I wouldn't have been with him in the first place. We shouldn't be held responsible for a violent thunderstorm. You and Father ought to be grateful that Carl got me safely to a shelter."

"Or should we be irate that he took advantage of an opportunity to be improperly intimate with you?"

"Mother!"

"The fact is that we can't know for sure, and neither can anyone else."

"Carl and I know, and our word should be good enough."

Amelia stood and put her arms on Lacy's shoulders in a sympathetic gesture. "Lacy, honey, you said yourself, Carl's a good man. He's certainly an attractive one. He is quite a catch, my dear. Several disappointed mothers of single daughters are lamenting right now that he's off the market. Try to be happy. You like each other, and that's more than some married couples can say. Love will grow between you, and I'm sure it'll happen soon." She hugged her. "And we know Carl is interested in you, or he wouldn't have invited you on a picnic in the first place. You're a smart, sweet, funny, clever girl. Just give him even half a chance to fall in love with you, and he'll be head over heels before the honeymoon's over."

Lacy took a deep breath. "I suppose so. I do enjoy his company. I just wish all these small-minded people wouldn't jump to the worst conclusion. He was a gentleman!"

"That's just how it is, dear. It isn't your fault. It isn't his, either. If anyone's at fault, the blame is mine. I shouldn't have begun allowing you to go out unescorted. But we can't undo that now. As your father would say, we have to play the hand we're dealt. You can turn it into a winning hand with your attitude. Now, put a smile on that pretty face. It's almost time for your father to walk you down the aisle."

"Unescorted, my hind foot. I would have gone with him anyway. I'm an adult now, Mother. I'm nineteen, in case you've forgotten. I'm old enough to make my own decisions."

"Oh, Lacy. That independent streak will cost you one day. I wish you would work on being more, well, obedient. More yielding."

"Apparently, I already am, or I wouldn't let myself be forced into this marriage." She gave Amelia a look that bordered on a defiant dare to be argued with. "Will Father come up to get me when they're ready?"

"Yes. I believe we're just waiting for the groom and best man. It's such a pity their parents couldn't attend. I hate that they're sick."

Lacy let out a mirthless chuckle. "Do you think it's a bad omen that the groom is late?"

"He'll kick himself when he sees how beautiful you are."

"Thank you, Mother." Lacy managed a smile.

"Are your bags all completely packed for your honeymoon in Cheyenne?"

"Yes. I have one bag packed for tonight at the hotel, then we catch the train east tomorrow. I'm glad it's a short trip from here to Cheyenne. You know how I don't like being cooped up for a long time on a moving train."

"Yes." Amelia laughed. "I'll never forget that regrettable train ride when we went to Chicago."

Lacy laughed at the memory. "Neither will the other passengers."

"I wonder what could be keeping your father. I'll go check." Amelia closed the door behind her as she left to go downstairs.

Their parlor had been transformed into a floral wonder-land. The pianist, a family friend, kept the attendees enter-tained with a wide assortment of songs. Even though it was a few minutes past time for the ceremony to start, people still had smiles on their faces and some even sang along to the music.

Amelia found her husband, George, waiting at the door. "What's the holdup?"

"Carl's nowhere to be found. I'll kill that scoundrel if he backs out now."

"That's not like him, I don't think. Surely, there's a good reason. I'll go back up to wait with Lacy. He'll be along soon; you'll see."

Upstairs, Lacy paced. "What could be keeping him? They don't live that far away."

"I'm sure it's nothing, Lacy," Amelia said, worry creeping into her voice.

"It's not like him, Mother."

"All we can do is wait, dear. I'm sure he'll be here soon, and I'll bet he'll have a good reason. Years from now when you tell your children about your wedding day, you'll both laugh about it."

Lacy thought about having children with Carl. Would she love him by then?

"Did you and Carl talk about whether or not you'd continue to work at the store with us after you're married?"

"We did. He decided to let me choose for myself. He said that should I become with child he'd prefer that I stay home. I agreed to that. Until then, I'm not sure yet. I'll probably work short days with you so I can take care of him and the house."

"That sounds like the perfect solution. We'll have time to find someone to work with us, and you can help us interview people. You see? He's a good man, to let you decide."

Lacy smiled ruefully. "We knew that already."

They heard sounds at the front door. Getting excited again, Amelia pinched Lacy's cheeks for color and told her to purse her lips a few times. Lacy stood in front of the full-length mirror, making sure everything was fine with the dress and veil.

The door opened and George appeared in the doorway along with a deputy sheriff. Gerald, Carl's brother, stood behind him in the hall.

"Carl's been found. Dead. Shot in the back."

ONE

The Big Rock Ladies' Aid Society was brought to order by the president, Harriet Smithers.

It was a specially scheduled meeting, called at the request of the minister's wife, Mrs. Charlotte Copperfield. Harriet turned the podium over to her.

"Thank you, Harriet. I know some of you have friends and relatives who are eager to move here to become brides and have been patiently waiting to be matched. Indeed, I know some are already in the process of corresponding with some of our townsmen." She paused for emphasis as she'd often seen her husband do during a sermon. "Ladies, I have what I consider to be an urgent need. The young woman in question, Lacy Hardy, attends the church in Laramie where Willis pastored before we came here. She was even in my Sunday School class. I know her and her family very well."

"How old is she?" Amy Larkin asked. Society meetings were very informal; the only adherence to their version of parliamentary procedure was Harriet's use of her gavel.

Charlotte stepped out from behind the podium, giving the audience the impression that her next words would be of greater import. She'd seen Willis use the technique many times.

"She's nineteen. Mind you, she's a good girl, but there was a scandal of sorts and it would be better if Lacy could start over in a new location. She's found herself ostracized since the incident."

"What was the incident?" Evie Glover asked.

"Yes, tell us about the scandal," Amy said.

"Well," Charlotte went on, "I wouldn't want you to get the wrong idea. The people in Laramie have scorned her. I don't want that happening here."

"Charlotte," Harriet said, "you know we aren't judgmental types in here. We won't think ill of Lacy."

"You might do well to remember that our last bride was about to be sent to prison for repeated thefts," Evie said, laughing. "That worked out fine, didn't it? She's one of us now."

"Yes, yes, of course, you're right," Charlotte said. "And truly, I believe the girl's word that nothing untoward happened. She and a young man had gone on an outing, a picnic, I believe. They had been seeing each other for four or five weeks, in town. Anyway, a horrible thunderstorm came out of nowhere. You know how it is in these mountains. Weather can hit in the blink of an eye. Trees were blown over and the horse spooked and ran. The young man found them shelter in an abandoned cabin just as the fiercest rains began to fall. That storm set in and stayed nearly all night. Early the next morning, they set out walking back to town. As you might expect, they looked quite haggard and unkempt when they arrived. The Hardys had guests, so soon other people knew they had spent the night together unchaperoned out in the wild. Lacy swears that she wasn't violated, but her parents insisted they marry to protect her reputation. The young man agreed to marry her."

"Then where's the scandal?" It was Evie butting in again.

"The young man didn't show up for the wedding. Lacy thought she'd been stood up until the deputy came and told them they had found the body of the groom. He'd been murdered."

Sympathetic murmurs arose around the room.

"Who killed him?" another woman asked.

"They don't know. Lacy herself has been suspected. It was speculated that she killed him so she wouldn't have to marry a man she didn't really love. To confound things, during the weeks he had been courting Lacy, he had apparently seen another young lady a time or two. She, too, fell under suspicion, but no evidence of wrongdoing on her part was found. It's all a most unfortunate situation. Certainly a tragedy for the young man, but now Lacy can't escape the shadow of impropriety on more than one level. The girl wasn't in love with him and would very much like to start over. I would dearly love to give her that chance, here in Big Rock."

There was chatter among the group. Finally Evie spoke for them. "Our own friends and relatives who are interested in coming here to marry aren't in dire circumstances. Our hearts are going out to your Lacy. Of course, we all want to welcome her to our community, and we're agreed that we should concentrate on finding a husband for her as soon as possible."

Charlotte gave them a grateful smile and put a hand on her heart in gratitude.

"All right," Harriet said, taking the podium again. "We certainly have enough bachelors to choose from. I've interviewed a few of them and have candidates in mind. First things first, though. Charlotte, if Lacy comes out here and isn't to be married immediately, will she stay in your home?"

"Yes, of course, we'd be delighted to sponsor her."

"Good," Harriet replied. "Now you've told us a little about

her situation, but what about the girl? What are her interests? What is her personality like?"

"Oh, all right. Well, she's nineteen and a smart girl. Reliable. Always studied her Sunday School lessons. She has a quick wit and a clever mind. Lacy works in her parents' store. She's a bit of an artist as I recall. I've seen her drawings. And she made some beautiful... well, I don't know what to call them," Charlotte said with a laugh. "They're like drawings or portraits, but she makes them out of fabric scraps on a muslin background. Up close, you can see the fabric scraps and they look a little rough and crude. But if you stand away and look at it, you can see the perfect likeness of a person or a landscape. Yes, she's an artist, definitely. She's basically a sweet girl at heart. Amelia, that's her mother, says she does have an independent streak, but that can be a healthy thing, don't you think?"

"It's healthy unless she really means to say the girl is rebellious. Or even unself-disciplined," Amy commented.

Evie and Harriet both chuckled aloud. Evie spoke up. "I don't think being unself-disciplined will be a problem for the men in this town. Most of them would be fully willing and prepared to apply some discipline to her *self* until she acquires some of her own."

The other women agreed with their own guffaws and giggles.

"All right, then," Harriet continued with her thoughts. "I have the names of a few men I've interviewed recently, but honestly, with the description Charlotte gave of Lacy, I have to believe Emmett Burke is our best candidate."

A chorus of *oh* went up from the ladies, drawn out and spoken with something akin to reverence.

"He is definitely an artist," Nessa Kelly said. "He made us a copper weathervane that's gorgeous. I've never seen another like it."

"He repaired our plow," Sandra Kinney said. "All right, that's not artistic, but he did a good job."

"Have you been in his blacksmith shop? He has all kinds of things he's made on display. Everything from horseshoes to belt buckles to copper pots. I swear, he can make anything made of metal." Lilac Indigo Reed nodded up and down, wide-eyed, as she looked around.

"And look mighty good while he's doing it, too," Shirley said.

"All right, I'll say it," Bethie Hickam said. "Let's face it, the man himself is a work of art." Bethie was perhaps the most free-spoken of the group.

"Oh my word, yes," Shirley Keller agreed. "The only good thing about the hot summer is seeing that man work over those smithy fires with no shirt on, only that leather apron covering him." Perhaps Shirley and Bethie were both the most outspoken.

Or maybe the honor belonged to Harriet. "I'll tell you a secret. I've requested special-made metal gifts from Arthur just so I can go with him to describe what I want to Emmett in person. I swear, he's almost as big and strong as Angus Kelly."

Nessa grinned with pride at that mention of her husband. At six foot eight, he was a giant in their town, a gentle, helpful, extremely strong giant of a man.

"Ladies," Charlotte cleared her throat, not so comfortable with the carnal direction their discussion had taken, "let's get back to business, please. What's the next step, Harriet?"

"I'll go immediately after this meeting, to see Emmett. If he's agreeable, then you know what we usually recommend is for Emmett to write to her and tell her about himself. Then she can write in return and they'll decide to pursue a union or not. Is there a reason you think that won't work?"

Charlotte looked anxious. "I just wish the process was

quicker. I'd like to get Lacy out of that situation tomorrow if I could."

"I suppose there's no reason why she can't go ahead and come to town and stay with you until they decide to marry. If they ultimately decide not to proceed, there are plenty of other men in town who would be interested. If he does want to marry her, I suspect he won't want to wait long. I tell you what. Let's see what Emmett says."

"I want to go with you to see him," Charlotte said.

"I do, too," several others said.

Harriet clicked her tongue and gave them a shaming look. "Ladies," she said scornfully, with a big, wicked grin on her face, "we don't want to overwhelm him. Charlotte and I will go."

"I'm ready," Charlotte said. The other ladies were too polite to say anything when they noticed the pastor's wife smooth down her hair and straighten her collar. They knew. They'd all seen Emmett.

HARRIET AND CHARLOTTE approached the blacksmith shop. Most of the people in town called it the blacksmith shop even though the official name of the business was Burke's Metal Works. That day, Emmett wore a shirt and Harriet was disappointed. It was hot in the front room even though all the windows were open for ventilation. There was some soot on his cheek and Harriet thought it might make him even more appealing. There was just such a masculine quality about him.

"Hello, Harriet, Mrs. Copperfield," Emmett said, flashing them a broad, toothy smile that had been known to, or at least thought to, melt the bloomers right off a woman.

"Emmett, you've been asking me to match you up with one

of our brides for a time now. Your wait paid off. We have the perfect woman for you," Harriet said.

Emmett put down the heavy tongs and picked up a towel to wipe his hands. "You have my full attention, ladies."

"The girl's name is Lacy Hardy and she's from Laramie. Charlotte knows her through their former church, where her husband pastored."

"A lovely girl," Charlotte said. "She was even in my Sunday School class."

Emmett nodded. "Tell me more," he said. "Tell me everything."

"Well," Harriet began, "there is a situation the poor girl is in. We want to get her away from there as quickly as we can."

"Is she in trouble? Or in danger?"

"Oh, no, Emmett, nothing like that. No danger. No trouble, exactly," Charlotte said, wavering on the last word.

"Well, what is it, exactly?" he asked.

Harriet took a deep breath and big leap of faith. "There was a young man who had begun to court her for a few weeks. They weren't in love but enjoyed talking and such. They went on a picnic out to a picturesque place near the river. An awful storm came up and frightened the horse and it ran away with the buggy. The storm intensified and the young man was forced to find them temporary shelter from the horrific winds and rains. It didn't let up until morning. I don't suppose I have to tell you that rumors tend to spread. It quickly came to the point where Lacy's father demanded the young man marry her. He agreed, even though neither of them wanted to marry. Then on the day of the wedding, he didn't show up. She thought she was being stood up, but it was much worse. He'd been murdered."

"Oh, no, that's terrible."

"It was, and it got worse. When authorities learned the two didn't want to get married, they tried to blame Lacy for the murder. Of course, there was no evidence, and she had a houseful of alibi witnesses, but the authorities kept investigating her. She was plagued by even more gossip. She became a pariah, and quickly. The cold accusing stares, the whispers, the turning away to avoid her. That's no way for a young woman to live. She just needs a fresh start. I believe you can give it to her."

"I could," he said. "But why me? Why did you pair her with me when I know there are other men in line before me?"

Charlotte smiled at him. "The girl is an artist in her own right. She draws and creates beautiful textile portraits. We all think of you as an artist, too. Your work is beautiful. We thought that would add a delightful dimension to your relationship."

Emmett laughed. "Ma'am, that's fanciful talk. I'm just a smithy."

"Now you're just being modest. Granted, there may not be much beauty to a horseshoe, but just look at some of these other pieces. It's a different kind of artistry, but it's still creative and beautiful."

"All right, maybe I can see that. I do enjoy making things. Tell me about her personality."

Charlotte beamed. "She's a good girl at heart. Sweet tempered, as I remember, and smart. Clever and witty, too."

"At heart? A good girl at heart?" he asked. "That sounds like it needs some explanation."

"Her mother tells me she's grown to have a mind of her own. Perhaps an independent streak. A small one." Charlotte held up her thumb and forefinger to illustrate a small amount.

Emmett nodded and stroked his chin thoughtfully. "I want a woman who has a mind of her own. Opinions of her own. Some spirit and a backbone. I'm not afraid of an independent streak. I can rein that in if I need to. All right, then, yes."

"Yes?" both ladies asked at the same time.

"Let's get her here as soon as we can. I'd like to marry her." He smiled. "As soon as we can."

"Wonderful!" Charlotte said. "And I promise you, she's still a virtuous girl. I believe her when she says she wasn't compromised."

"That's a wonderful thing and something to be treasured, but really, I'd marry her either way. What she did before me doesn't matter. After all, I haven't exactly led a celibate life. What matters is what happens from now on."

Charlotte colored a little bit and Harriet tittered at the thought of the possible number of women he hadn't been celibate with.

"Emmett, you haven't even asked what she looks like. Don't you wonder?" Harriet asked.

Emmett laughed and it was a deep, hearty sound. "Yes, ma'am, I do, more than you can imagine. But Miz Charlotte said she's lovely and I was afraid I'd seem shallow if I asked about her looks."

Harriet joined him in the laugh. "Tell him everything you know, Charlotte."

"Lacy is indeed a lovely young woman. Her coloring is much like your own; she has dark wavy hair and hazel eyes. Such a nice smile, it lights up a room, as they say."

"Tell him what he wants to know, Charlotte. What kind of figure does she have?"

"I haven't seen her since we moved here, but she had a, um, nice figure, as I recall." Charlotte's hands went up in front of her, then fell, then went up again before she doubled them up in fists and frowned.

"Are you trying to say she's a buxom girl?" Harriet asked.

"I'm trying my best not to say it," Charlotte said, looking down in embarrassment. "Oh! Amelia, that's Lacy's mother, did mention Lacy would wear the wedding gown she had been married in. They didn't even have to make alterations. Her mother always had a fine figure. What they call an hourglass figure."

Emmett stroked his chin again, a smile spreading across his face.

"I'll definitely marry her. Give me the information I need, and I'll wire money for her fare tomorrow. Find out how soon she can get here. I see no reason to delay, do you?"

"Are you sure you don't want to get to know her first?"

He grinned *that grin* again. "I'll get to know her pretty well after we're married. Of course, there's always the possibility she won't want to marry me."

Harriet chuckled. "No, there's not. I can't imagine a woman not wanting to marry you, Emmett."

"Harriet," he said, putting his arm around her shoulder, "you are a shameless flirt. Does Arthur know you talk to men like this?"

"Yes, he does. And he's very appreciative once I get home, if you know what I mean."

Emmett laughed again and Charlotte buried her face in her hands.

"I forgot to ask one thing. How old is Lacy?"

"Nineteen," Harriet answered. "Is that too young for you?"

"I'm twenty-eight. Do you think I'm too old for her?"

"Not a bit. All right, Emmett, I'll bring you the information you need tomorrow, to send money to her. We're about to head over to Caleb's and send her a wire about you. Anything you want us to say on your behalf?"

"Yes, ma'am. Tell her I want to marry her the day she arrives. And I look forward to it very much."

HARRIET AND CHARLOTTE hurried to Caleb Carter's telegraph and newspaper office. On the way, they discussed what to say in the wire. How do you tell a woman about a man like Emmett and convey everything you really want to say? Charlotte composed the message.

COME *to Big Rock as soon as you can get here* STOP *Found husband for you* STOP *Emmett Burke* STOP *He will wire fare money tomorrow* STOP *He asks you to marry him* STOP *He looks forward to it* STOP *Get here* STOP *He is amazing* STOP *Handsome* STOP *Emmett wants to marry the day you arrive* STOP *Trust me* STOP *Do it* STOP *My goodness make haste* STOP *If you never do anything else I say do this* STOP *Marry the man* STOP *Wire back as soon as possible* STOP *Charlotte Copperfield*

"CHARLOTTE," Harriet said. "That's going to be an expensive wire to send."

"I'll take money out of the collection plate if I have to."

"Charlotte!"

TWO

Laramie, Wyoming Territory

Amelia watched as her daughter packed her bags, separating her belongings into piles of things to be packed into carpetbags to travel with her, things to be packed in large suitcases to go in the baggage car, and things to be shipped to her later in trunks and crates.

"Lacy, are you sure you want to go out there and marry that man, sight unseen? That's awfully foolish."

"I want to start over, Mother. Away from here. Big Rock is far enough away from the scandal, and close enough that you can come visit. It's the perfect solution."

"I can understand moving; your father and I have no problem with that. But marriage? To someone you don't love?"

Lacy stopped what she was doing and looked at her mother. "Have you forgotten you and father were insistent that I marry a man I didn't love only weeks ago?"

"Well, that was different. Much different! We were confident love would grow between you and Carl."

"And I'm confident love will grow between me and

Emmett. Miz Charlotte assures me he's a fine man, and he certainly sounds like quite a catch."

"But why marry so soon? Why not stay with the Copperfields until you decide you're sure about marrying him?"

"I'm already sure, Mother."

"But I worry so, dear."

Lacy sat down on the bed beside Amelia. "I have an idea. Why don't you come out there with me? I'm sure the Copperfields would love to have you visit them for a few days. You can meet Emmett for yourself and calm your worries. Travel shouldn't take that long. Surely, Father can handle the store for a few days without you."

"Oh, I don't know. It would be in poor taste to invite myself out there, don't you think?"

"I don't think so. Hasn't Charlotte been inviting you to visit ever since they moved?"

"Well, yes, I guess she has."

"I think she'd love to see you. And I'd love to have you at my wedding." Lacy grinned at her mother with a hint of mischief. "I'd invite you to stay with us, but under the circumstances, it might not be practical."

"Lacy!" Amelia said, then she giggled a little. "You're probably right. My sweet Lacy, would you like to talk about your wedding night? I should have had this talk with you before you were to marry Carl, but I couldn't bring myself to say the words."

"Oh," Lacy said as she exhaled a deep breath.

"I wish I had been more prepared for mine," Amelia said as a means of encouragement. "Your father was good with me; he was patient and I sort of understood and got the hang of it. I had no idea what would happen. We didn't talk of these things back in those days. I was as frightened and timid as a kitten."

"To be honest, I don't know exactly what to expect, but I'm

not frightened." She looked ruefully at her mother. "I might be when the time comes, though."

"Maybe Emmett's the kind of man who won't press you until you're ready. Until you get to know him better."

"Maybe, but we know he's the kind of man who wants to marry immediately, so we could reason that he's not one to wait on, you know, that," Lacy said.

Amelia smiled. "Then perhaps we should talk about 'that'. I'll tell you what I can, but truthfully, I can't imagine going to bed with a man I only met that day, even if we were legally wed. With your father, I already knew I was fond of him."

"I wonder about what that'll be like, too." She paused. "At least I know he's a handsome man, so I shouldn't mind being... close."

"True, but I hope Charlotte's right and there's more to him than his looks. Handsome people can be ugly inside. But I don't think she'd steer you wrong. And I certainly hope you find joy in being close. I didn't, my first time. I think I was just too scared. But in time, I found physical fulfillment."

"Was it painful your first time? I've heard it can be."

Amelia smiled. "It felt something like a pinch, but it wasn't that bad. Your father was nervous, too. There was fumbling. I suspect it wouldn't have hurt if we'd taken more time before-hand for my body to be ready for him." Her smile grew wider. "Young love. Sometimes it makes a man overly eager."

"I have to think a man like Emmett has experience... in these things. That's a safe assumption, given Miz Charlotte's description of him. I'd like to know how many women there have been."

"No, Lacy, you don't. Promise me you'll never ask."

"Why?"

"Well, for one thing, you don't want to come across as a jealous shrew. For another thing, well, just be grateful that his life's experiences have made him the man he is today. You can't hold him accountable for his life prior to you."

"I suppose so. I'll always wonder, though."

"Wonder all you want. But keep it to yourself. Better yet, don't think about it. It'll only make you jealous and miserable. It'll make you both miserable."

"All right, all right."

"Why don't we make a trip to Handel's Dress Shop and buy you some new dainties? Maybe a nice, special nightgown to wear on your wedding night," Amelia said.

Lacy grinned. "I guess that means we're giving up on the thought that he's the kind of man who would be willing to wait for *that*."

"Yes, I believe so. And while we're out, we'll wire Charlotte and let her know I'm coming to visit. Then I need to get back and pack, too. Come on! We need to hurry."

———

THEY LEFT the telegraph office and went directly to Handel's Dress Shop. The shop had an extensive line of clothing and accessories for women. Lacy went straight to the lingerie section and picked up and examined several styles of bloomers. She was surprised there was such an extensive assortment. Lacy decided against the plain and practical ones and stepped over to the pretty ones. Most had lace trim and dainty ribbon flowers, some had embroidery, but the ones that caught her eye had lace inserts. There were set-in sections of peekaboo lace in diamond shapes on the fabric. Another pair was similar, but it had a soft, sheer lining behind the lace that was barely opaque. She wondered if Emmett enjoyed seeing a woman in such things. She smiled as she collected several pairs and handed them to the saleswoman.

The shifts were nearby, and she selected three of them. They were more feminine than the ones she usually wore, but not as fanciful as the bloomers. They would be fine.

Next, she went to the rack of nightwear. Lacy marveled at the selection; she saw everything from long, full, flannel gowns to shorty little things made of delicate, gossamer-thin silk. She picked up a silk one to look at it more closely.

Amelia came over to join her. "I picked out a new dress to wear at your wedding. Whoa! Look at that. Not very much to it, is there?"

"Not much. I wonder how hard it is to launder."

Amelia laughed. "Lacy, honey, you don't consider lingerie like that if you're concerned about laundry. Its purpose is far and away removed from that."

"I know the purpose, Mother, but at some point it will have to be cleaned."

"Well, see if they have something similar in cotton. You know how to wash that."

"Oh, look, they do have some thin cotton ones that are almost as pretty. Do you like this one?" She held it up against herself.

"It looks like it would be revealing. I think it's safe to say most men would like it. Quite a bit."

"I think I'll get it. Maybe a couple of others, too. I think I like this pink one. It's a little longer, nearly mid-thigh. Oh, look at this one. It opens all the way down the front. Aren't these little ribbon bows pretty?"

"Lacy, honey, get two like that. I imagine your man will enjoy untying them."

She got the one with the delicate ties and another one with buttons.

"I hate to even mention it, but you might want to get at least one of those flannel ones. It is cold in Wyoming, you know. Besides, there are those times every month when these little fripperies just won't do. I'm sure we can find a pretty one that won't make you feel like either a small child or an old lady."

"You're right. I don't think I'll buy a robe. Do you think the one I have is nice enough?"

"Probably. You could opt for those peignoir sets over there. I have to tell you, though, I never really liked them. They're attractive enough, but that little covering doesn't actually cover anything. If anyone else is in the house, you still have to put on a heavier robe over it."

"I think I have enough now." Lacy laughed. "More than enough. I might need another carpetbag."

THAT AFTERNOON when the ladies arrived back home after their big shopping day, they carried all of Lacy's things up to her room. Amelia had only bought a dress and several pairs of stockings. She dropped them off in her room on the way to Lacy's.

They heard voices downstairs. "Were you expecting visitors, Mother?"

"No. Who is your father talking to? That's not a friendly conversation."

Lacy flew down the stairs, followed by her mother. The uninvited visitor and the person on the other end of the heated discussion was the same deputy sheriff who had come on the day of the wedding.

"You need to leave my house right now, Deputy."

"I need to speak to Miss Hardy."

"I'm here," she said as she walked up to stand beside her father.

"What do you know of a woman named Heather Matthews?"

"She's a member of our church. Why?"

"It's come to light in our investigation that Carl Nixon was seeing her the same time he was courting you. Did you know that?"

"No, I didn't. What difference does it make now? The man's dead."

"Maybe you found out about her and killed him for two-timing you."

"Deputy Faust, you know the story of what happened. I know you know the rumors. Carl and I were not in love. Even if he had been seeing someone else, I wouldn't have cared. Besides, you've already talked to several people who were with me at the time. I can't be in two places."

"That's what accomplices are for. You'd better keep in mind that we're watching you."

"Watch me all you want in the next day, Deputy. I'm moving the day after that."

"I'm afraid you can't do that. It's an active investigation."

"Yes, of a murder I had nothing to do with." She squared her shoulders and pushed out her chest and folded her arms in front of it. "If you want to talk to me after tomorrow, I'll be in Big Rock. You can wire me."

"Maybe this Heather woman found out about Lacy and she killed Carl. Did you think about that possibility?" Mr. Hardy asked.

The deputy just stared at him. The Hardys couldn't tell if he wanted to refute that idea or if he hadn't thought of it.

Deputy Faust left.

"Father, you know Heather would never kill anyone."

"I know, but I know you wouldn't, either."

They had all three turned and headed to the kitchen when

there was another knock on the door. "Now who the devil could that be?" Mr. Hardy said to no one in particular as he went back to the door and opened it.

It was another member of their church. He took off his hat before speaking.

"We're just letting everyone know that Clive and Mamie Nixon have passed away. She went late last night, and he followed her a few hours later. They got that sickness and just never got better. After Carl died, I think they just didn't want to. Poor Gerald, he's the only one left now. So much death in that family recently."

"When is the funeral?" Amelia asked.

"Day after tomorrow, at noon."

"Oh, Lacy and I can't be there, I'm afraid. We'll be on a train by then."

"I'll go," George Hardy said. "I'll just close up the store for a while."

The family was quiet as Amelia and Lacy put supper on the table.

"I wonder what Gerald will do now? He moved out quite some time ago," Amelia said.

"Why exactly did he move, Father? I never knew. I didn't want to ask Carl and he didn't offer to talk about it."

"I don't know for sure. I think there may have been some family disagreement. Of course, sometimes men just move out because they want to strike out on their own to be independent."

"Well, that's a true statement. Whereas if I were to move out on my own, my virtue would be questioned," Lacy said.

George gave his daughter an indulgent smile. "We've had this discussion before, princess. That's just the way it is. Always has been, always will be."

The idea that it had to be that way rankled, but it was softened by his use of her pet name *princess*. He hadn't called her that in a long time.

GEORGE TOOK Lacy and Amelia to the train while it was still dark; it was an early departure.

"Lacy, princess, I wish I could be there to give you away, but I can't leave the store for that long. This has all happened so fast!"

"I know, Father, I wish you could be there, too. But it's not going to be any big affair, so you won't miss much."

"To a father, it's very much. Now, princess, I hope you know this already, but if for any reason, any reason at all, you want to come home, you just have to wire me. I'll move Heaven and Earth to get you on the next stage and train back here."

"I do know that. I promise we'll come visit as soon as we can. Maybe when you get a new employee hired, you'll be able to take some time and visit us."

"I would like that. I'd like to see your new home. I want to see you happy."

Lacy tiptoed and kissed her father on the cheek.

"Amelia, you take care of our baby," he said as he kissed her. "And get yourself back here safely. Tell the Copperfields I send my best. Have a good visit. Both of you, have a safe trip."

THE LADIES SHARED a Pullman unit on the train. That evening after the dinner stop and just before they decided to change for sleep, Lacy turned more introspective. "I've always heard that a happy marriage happens when best friends marry. Do you think that's true?"

"I wholeheartedly agree. Your father and I were friends who fell in love. And as our love grew, so did our friendship." She laughed. "It's most convenient to have your friend and your lover occupy the same body."

"I hope it doesn't put Emmett and me at a disadvantage that we haven't been friends before now."

"I don't think it has to put you at a disadvantage. When you get down to it, you're really only lovers a small percentage of the time. In those non-relation times, develop that friendship. Play. Play a lot, Lacy. I've found that a common sense of humor is a wonderful tool for developing a closeness. Who doesn't love to laugh?"

"I hope he likes to laugh. Surely, Miz Charlotte wouldn't have been so eager for us to get together if he were a dour man."

"I wouldn't worry about that. He sounds like a fine man."

"What if he doesn't like my cooking?"

Amelia laughed. "Sweetheart, that's what that flimsy night-ie's for. You wear that, and he'll be happy to eat jerky and hard-tack. In the meantime, you can learn how he likes his roasts and steaks cooked."

Lacy let her insecurity show up again. "Mother?"

"Yes?"

"What if Emmett isn't satisfied with our relations?"

Amelia laughed. "Don't say 'no' to anything he wants to do, and you'll have a very happy man."

"What do you mean, anything he wants to do?"

"Men tend to like to vary things. Remember what I said about being willing to play to develop strength in your relation-ship? That applies to your intimate relationship, too. Be play-ful. Be willing. He will be wild about you. And wildly devoted. He'll love you more than you can imagine."

"I hope you're right."

"I am, dear. Cherish it while you can."

Lacy noticed the faraway look in her mother's eye; it seemed to have a hint of sadness.

"Mother? Mother, what's bothering you?"

"Oh, Lacy," she said as she took Lacy's hand in hers. "You're old enough now, about to be a married woman. I suppose it's natural for us to become friends as well as mother and daughter."

"I would treasure your friendship, just as I treasure having you as a mother. Tell me what's suddenly made you so sad?"

"Well, it's not really sudden. When I said to cherish your physical relationship while you can, I meant it. You know when your father had that fever a couple of years ago, it affected him. Since then, he hasn't been able to, well, perform as a man."

"Mother, I had no idea. I'm not sure what to say."

Amelia smiled. "I don't suppose there is anything to say. I always knew that ardor wanes as we age. I just didn't expect it to happen so soon in our lives. It bothers your father deeply. He doesn't even seem to want to be close anymore, like cuddling the way we used to. I think it reminds him of his inability to pleasure me the way he did before, to pleasure both of us. He must surely miss it himself, but he won't speak of it."

"You're both so young still. You know, I would never have known if you hadn't told me."

Amelia patted her hand and smiled again. "That's because we're still friends. We still enjoy being together, in each other's company."

"But you're still such a vibrant woman." Lacy drifted off into her own world of thoughts when Amelia seemed not to want to talk about it anymore.

THREE

Big Rock, Wyoming Territory

Amelia helped Lacy freshen up as the stagecoach neared Big Rock. Lacy was nervous, and Amelia shared that even she was a little anxious. She felt sure the Copperfields would be there to greet them and that was comforting.

Emmett. She was just minutes away from meeting the man with whom she'd spend the rest of her life.

She closed her eyes. *Dear Lord, please, if this is a mistake and it's not in your will for me to marry Emmett, give me some sign. Or a sign if it is in your will. If this marriage is to be, please give me the conviction and confidence I need to be sure. In His name, Amen.*

Her mother was looking at her when she looked up, and Amelia took her hand. "I said a prayer for you, too."

The coach rumbled to a stop and Lacy took a deep breath. She heard a hand on the door latch at the same time she heard someone climb the ladder on the back of the coach up to the top where the baggage was tied. The door opened. There were a few people outside, but she couldn't focus on any of them because the people who were nearer the door were in her line of vision. She stood as soon there was room, then her mother stood. She looked at the floor as she made her way to the coach door to make sure she didn't stumble. She finally looked up when she stood in the doorway.

Oh sweet Jesus.

"Lacy. Welcome home." Emmett didn't help her step down. He reached up and put his hands at her waist and lifted her down. His eyes never left hers.

Those eyes. That mouth. The smile. Say something back to him.

"It's good to be here." Was that her own voice? It sounded so nervous to her ears.

He put her down but kept his left hand on her waist as he turned to give Amelia help negotiating the coach steps. Lacy looked up at this gorgeous man as he helped her mother and noted that she seemed taken with him, too. Charlotte Copperfield ran to Amelia and hugged her, and Emmett turned back to Lacy.

"Let's step over here." He guided her away from the bustle immediately, around the stage. "It seems like I've waited so long for you to arrive. Doesn't it seem to you like it's been more than just a few days?"

Lacy managed to smile, grateful that he was making conversation. "So much has happened in so short a time."

"I hope you had a good trip."

"It was pleasant. But I am glad it's over. I didn't realize stagecoach rides were so bumpy."

"Lacy," he looked directly into her eyes and there was no way she could possibly have looked away, "will you marry me today?"

Breathe. Remember to breathe.

"Yes."

She'd lived her entire life to see the look he gave her. He stepped a little closer to her and leaned down to kiss her forehead.

"I think the plan is for all of us to go across the street to Mary's Restaurant to eat. Then we'll go to the parsonage and the ladies can help you get changed into your dress and get freshened up while the men go on and wait for you at the church. Does that sound all right to you?"

"It sounds fine. What about after the ceremony?" She wondered if there would be a short time for visiting with the Copperfields and Amelia.

He put his finger under her chin and tilted her head up to look at him. His voice softened. "That's when I take you home with me. I want you all to myself."

No, I'm pretty sure he's not the type of man who'll give me time before he'll want relations.

Lacy identified the bags that belonged to her and her mother. Emmett took them when they were handed down to him by the man on top of the coach and put them in his wagon. She watched Emmett as he moved, struck by the way the muscles across his back and shoulders and arms flexed, even through his shirt.

When the bags were loaded, Emmett said the wagon would be fine where it was until they had eaten. The restaurant was just across the street and the wagon would be within their view. With that charming smile beguiling them, he put one arm around Lacy and held out his other for Amelia to take.

The seven of them sat down at a long table. Emmett sat on the end, Lacy next to him, and Amelia beside her daughter. The Copperfields and the Smitherses sat on the opposite side. Emmett's arm rested on the back of Lacy's chair, and occasionally she felt his touch. She seemed so acutely aware of it that in her mind, the heat branded her.

"Amelia, I can't tell you how good it is to see you and Lacy," Charlotte Copperfield said, repeating what she'd said when she first saw them. "I wish George could have come."

"He does, too, but there was no way he could close the store for so long. He sends you his love. He told me to tell you, Willis, that when he does come out here for a visit, he's going to want a chance to redeem himself after that day when you caught fourteen trout and he pulled in bare hooks all day."

"Tell him I know just the place," the reverend answered.

"There's a great spot just behind my cabin," Emmett said. "I'll have to tell Mr. Hardy my secret, so he won't lose again."

Willis laughed. "Look at you, Emmett! It might not be wise to conspire against a man of God."

"Possibly so, but it also seems prudent to join forces with my father-in-law. Besides, I'll catch more than both of you, anyway," he said and winked at Lacy.

That wink. That look. His arm around me. That smile. Those lips. Those muscles.

All those things, those flashes of awareness of him swirled in her head. She shyly smiled back at him and caught the twinkle in his eye.

Eyes. Lips. I'll be kissing those lips.

When their food arrived, Emmett removed his arm from the back of her chair and Lacy felt the loss. She realized that for an instant she had an intense jealousy of the cutlery he picked up with *those hands.*

Soon those hands will hold me. Touch me. What will his touch feel like?

The others commented on how good Mary's food was, but she barely tasted it as she ate. Her mind was on being back at his cabin after the wedding. *What will it be like? How will he be with me? Will he be courtly? Gentle? Rough? Patient? Insis-*

*tent? Forceful? Will he expect me to know things I don't? Will
he tell me what he wants me to do? Show me?*

"Lacy," Harriet said, "I can't wait for you to see some of the
beautiful work Emmett's done."

Lacy turned her head to Emmett with a curious look. "Are
you an artist?" she asked him.

He laughed, shaking his head. "I'm a blacksmith."

Charlotte and Harriet both chuckled. "Don't let him kid
you, child. Emmett's quite a talented man. He's our blacksmith,
all right, but he's also a silversmith and coppersmith and
tinsmith, too. He's a wizard with any kind of metal. The man
can make everything from horseshoes to the finest jewelry and
accent pieces."

She looked at him with a new respect, pleased and a little
awed at the same time. "I didn't know that," she said. "I can't
wait to see some of your work."

"Emmett," Charlotte said, "you should take Lacy to see your
shop on the way out of town."

Arthur and Willis grinned, and even Harriet chuckled. "I'm
sure he'll take her to see it in time."

"I promise I will. I closed the shop for a few days," he said,
his eyes hinting at his intentions to get her alone soon. "Besides,
you can see some of my work at the cabin. I made some things
especially for it. Miz Charlotte said you're an artist, too. Did
you bring some pieces with you? I look forward to seeing what
you do. It sounds interesting."

"I brought a couple of my favorites. Father will ship the rest
with my things later."

"They're quite nice," Charlotte said. "I'm sure her work has
gotten even better in the years since I last saw it. And it was
striking then."

"Amelia," Harriet began, "it's been such a pleasure meeting

you and getting to know you. Do you have any idea how long you'll be staying with us?"

Amelia looked at Charlotte, not sure how to answer. They hadn't discussed it.

Charlotte spoke up. "We're hoping you can stay at least two or three weeks, even longer if you like. I'm sure you'll want to see Lacy settled down with Emmett."

"Oh, I can't leave George to handle the store for that long by himself. I was thinking more like four or five days, at the most. I mostly wanted to keep Lacy company on the trip and meet Emmett and, of course, visit with my dear friends."

Charlotte looked a little let down. "Well, let's keep it open. Maybe in a couple of days, you can wire George and see how he's doing, then you'll be comfortable staying longer."

Emmett put his arm back around Lacy. "Mrs. Hardy, I hope you'll be able to stay a bit longer. I'm sure you understand I'd like to have Lacy to myself for a couple of days, but I hope you can visit with us a while, too. I know you'll want to see where Lacy lives. You and your husband are always welcome." He flashed that smile again. "I even have a special guest room set up for you. Visit anytime. Well," he added, "any time after two or three days."

Amelia was touched. "Emmett, please call me Amelia. And thank you, yes, I'd love to see Lacy's new home."

Mary's offer of dessert was turned down, with everyone agreeing they wanted to get to a wedding.

Emmett helped Amelia up onto his wagon seat then walked around to the other side. Lacy felt like the smile he gave her was special, as though it was a different smile reserved for her only. It was nonsense, of course, but he made her feel that way. That tingly butterfly feeling hadn't left her since she first saw him.

"It's not far from here, just down that street and over one.

You can see the church steeple from here." He pointed it out. "It's the only church in town. There was talk of building a Presbyterian one, but the plans fell through."

"It seems like a nice little town," Amelia offered.

"I liked it enough to settle here," Emmett said.

"Where are you from originally?" Lacy asked.

"I was born just outside of Cheyenne. My father was a blacksmith there and I grew up working with him. When he died, I sold everything and moved. I even lived in Laramie for a while. Just think, we might have passed each other on the street before."

No, I would remember you.

"I don't know, Laramie's a pretty big city," she said.

"So, your mother has passed on, too?" Amelia asked.

"Yes, ma'am. She died when I was fifteen."

"Do you have any siblings?"

"I did. I had a little brother, Billy. He drowned in a pond when he was four. I don't have many memories of him."

"I'm so sorry, Emmett," Amelia said.

"Thank you, but it was a long time ago. No more sad talk now. This is a happy day," Emmett said.

"Yes, it is," Amelia agreed.

The parsonage was next door to the church. There was a large place for wagons and buggies on the other side of the church, and there was a cemetery behind them both. Emmett pulled his wagon up beside the buggies that belonged to the pastor and the Smitherses.

Amelia started to get down, but Emmett jumped down and ran around the wagon. "Wait! Let me help you down," he said. "Give me a chance to make a good impression." Amelia was charmed and thought that was endearing.

He lifted Lacy down much the same way he'd lifted her down from the stage. Perhaps more slowly this time, though.

"Tell me which bags go in here and which ones go on home."

———

"OH, that dress is beautiful. It fits you so perfectly, Lacy," Charlotte said. "You'd think it was made for you."

Amelia laughed. "It was made for me, and I couldn't fasten it without a corset so tight I could barely breathe. Look at that tiny waist. It fits her perfectly." She stood back. "You look beautiful, Lacy. You're a stunning bride."

"All right, Lacy, let's see now, your dress can be something old. I think I have something that could work for both something borrowed and something blue." She searched through one of the drawers in a high, narrow chest. "Would you like to wear these?" Charlotte held up a pair of lace gloves with a pale blue ribbon woven through the wrist. They were ideal with the dress.

"Yes, they're perfect!" Lacy answered. "Will my new undies count as something new?"

"I don't see why not," Charlotte said. "Now sit down and let us tidy that hairdo and get this veil on."

———

AMELIA HELD Lacy's hand as they walked to the church next door.

"Let me go on in and see if they're ready," Charlotte said. "I asked Nessa Kelly to play the *Wedding March* on the piano. Our usual pianist is out of town. I hope that's all right."

"Of course," Lacy said. "That would be nice."

"You'll love Nessa. She was our first mail order bride," Charlotte said with a little pride in her voice. "I'll be back in a minute. Wait here."

Amelia turned to her daughter. "Do you have any last minute jitters?"

"Mother, I don't have any jitters at all. Everything seems... right."

"It does, doesn't it? It would have been nice if your father could be here."

"I have him in here." Lacy patted her heart. "Maybe you need to remember what you taught me when I was a child. You just can't have everything you want."

Amelia smiled. "You are right. Besides, Emmett was right. Today is a happy day. We'll have no sad thoughts creeping in." She reached up and brought down the portion of the veil that falls on the face. Lacy could still see; it was a very delicate, thin lace.

Charlotte came back out then. "Nessa's going to start playing in a moment, and you can walk in as soon as you're ready. Amelia, would you like to go in with me?"

"No, wait," Lacy said. "Walk in with me. It will be almost like you're walking me down the aisle like Father would have."

Charlotte nodded and went inside. The music began and they linked arms to walk in. When Lacy saw her groom, she wondered where the suit jacket had come from. She hadn't noticed it in the wagon, but then, she'd been nervous and probably missed several things. Lacy couldn't keep from smiling at him, and he returned it. When they reached the front, Amelia blew Lacy a kiss since the veil covered her face. She released her arm and stood aside next to Charlotte.

Lacy could scarcely pay attention to the minister's words; all she could think about was what it would be like when they got home. She wondered if it was a sin to think about those things in a church, but she couldn't keep from it. Fortunately, she paid enough attention so that she responded appropriately when it was her turn to say something.

When the minister asked if there were rings to be exchanged, she was about to say, "No," when she heard Emmett say, "Yes."

He reached into his pocket and pulled out two silver rings, one larger than the other. He handed her the large one so she could put it on his finger when the time came. "Sorry," he whispered, "I forgot to give it to you beforehand."

When the time came and he placed a ring on her finger, it was a perfect fit. She looked up at him, very pleased that it did. He must have read her mind because he reached into the breast pocket of his jacket, out of view of the others, and produced two other rings that were identical to hers, but in different sizes. She had to stifle a giggle.

Finally the time came when Reverend Copperfield told Emmett he could now kiss his bride.

Emmett slowly pulled the veil up and over the top of her head, revealing her face. He put his hands around her head under the fall of the veil, his fingers toward the back of her head and his thumbs on her cheeks, caressing them. He gently pulled up and Lacy followed his lead and tiptoed. He leaned down and kissed her, softly and sweetly, and only a heartbeat too long for propriety.

The minister introduced them as Mr. and Mrs. Emmett Burke and the applause and shouts from the few assembled there made them smile. Everyone congratulated them, hugging and kissing and handshaking all around.

Outside, there were last minute hugs from the women and plans were made for Amelia to come spend the night with Lacy and Emmett in three days' time. Lacy and Emmett would come get her and she would stay with them until time for her to leave for Laramie. She hadn't finalized her return trip yet.

Emmett lifted Lacy up onto the seat of the wagon. At the last minute, she remembered to give the gloves back to Charlotte. Then they were off.

Emmett placed his hand on her thigh and squeezed. "I sure am glad you didn't back out."

The forge in his shop couldn't be any hotter than his hand.

"No, I never even considered it," she said as she smiled back at him. "I prayed for the strength of my conviction if this was the right thing to do, and once we met, it just felt right."

They were strong-sounding words, but it took every bit of her will to say them. Inside, she quaked, the thought of them becoming intimate beginning to unnerve her.

"It does feel right." He squeezed her thigh again.

On the way out of town, he drove by his shop and pointed it out.

"That's a big place. The blacksmith shop Father uses in Laramie is a lot smaller."

"It started smaller, but I wanted to be able to work with all kinds of metals, and different kinds require some different tools and processes. Plus, I like to spread out when I work and have plenty of room. I tend to work on more than one thing at a time. I'll show it to you soon. Who knows? You may like it so much, you'll want to apprentice." He laughed and she enjoyed the sound of it. It warmed her somehow.

After a moment of quiet, Emmett broke the silence. "I thought that was a nice little ceremony. Did you?"

Brought out of her reverie, Lacy remembered something she wanted to ask him. She said it with excitement that seemed to please him. "Did you really make our wedding bands? They're beautiful." She held up her hand to admire it again.

"I did. I was so afraid you wouldn't like them. I'd be ashamed to tell you how many designs I tried before I settled on that one."

"Really? You were worried?"

"Of course, I was. I wanted them to be perfect. I wanted you to like them."

"Emmett, I love them, and I love that you made them yourself. They couldn't be any better."

He grinned. "Well, I'll tell you something else about them. Let me give you a quick history lesson. And a little geology lesson, too."

Lacy looked up at him, wondering what he could possibly be talking about.

"Big Rock grew up around a silver mine, southeast of town. It's long since been mined out, but it was a big, bustling concern in its day. I don't know how much you know about silver, but it doesn't look like that in the ground." He pointed at his ring. "It usually forms in and with other ores, usually in a lead ore called galena. Copper and sometimes even gold ores are found with it. Mostly, though, it's with lesser known ores that still have value, but not like silver and gold. The silver has to be extracted from the chunks of ore. Pure silver is too soft to make anything from it, so it's mixed with nickel to harden it. Anyway, one of the first settlers in the area discovered the ore when he was trying to dig a well for water. By himself, he managed to mine a good deal of ore. He called the biggest chunk of it the *big rock*. When he claimed the land and needed people to come work for him at the time, he was faced with naming the town. There were already several Silver Cities, so that was out. He called it Big Rock, and he saved that original chunk of ore instead of processing it. I know the man who still has that big rock, and I persuaded him to let me hack off a piece of it so I could extract the silver. So you and I, Lacy, are wearing rings that contain a little piece of the rock that built the town."

Her mouth widened with awe as did her eyes. "Emmett, is that true?"

"Every word of it, darlin'."

"How do you know the man with the rock?"

"He's my uncle, Gann Douglas. He lives outside of town on the other side of the old mine."

"Well, how did he come by the rock?"

"His father, my grandfather, was the man who owned the mine. Gann and my mother inherited when my granddad passed away." Emmett looked at her and grinned again. "You, darlin', by most standards, are a rich woman now."

"No, you're joking with me. Charlotte would have mentioned that, surely."

"She probably doesn't know. It's not a secret, but most people probably don't know or haven't put two and two together and figured it out. The people who do know probably don't realize quite how much money it is."

"How... how much money is it?"

"A lot. Enough that our children will inherit and be very grateful to their great-grandpa."

"I won't have spoiled children. They'll work and have responsibilities like other children," she said with conviction.

"I agree with you completely. And we have enough that I never have to worry about making a living. I work because I like to. I mean, I have to do something with my time." He furrowed his brow slightly in thought. "Although I might work less now that I have something else to do with my time."

The look he gave her made it clear to her that she was the something else. Her thoughts of intimacies surfaced again.

"That was a nice kiss at the wedding," she said softly. She looked down and then back up at him again. "It was my first kiss."

"Really? Your first? I'm honored that I could be your first, Lacy. That's a gift I hadn't expected. What about your beau? That man you were caught with in that storm?"

"Oh, Carl? No, we weren't romantic. I never felt," Lacy looked up at Emmett with a little embarrassment at what she was about to say, "with him the way you make me feel."

He squeezed her leg again, a little higher. "We can explore that feeling a little later. Right now, I can't imagine a man seeing you for weeks without trying to at least steal a kiss."

She waved her hand dismissively. "Oh no. Besides, his friend Alan was always there. Those two were inseparable."

A suspicion gnawed at Emmett. "Carl was never alone with you?" He couldn't understand why any red-blooded man wouldn't want to be alone with Lacy.

"No," she laughed, "Alan wouldn't leave us alone. They were such cut ups." Her smile faded just a little. "Alan was even supposed to go on that picnic with us that day, but he got sick. If he'd gone, things would have been different, I imagine."

"Then I'm awfully glad the man got sick, or I wouldn't have you now."

She put her hand on his thigh. It was low on his thigh, but it was on his thigh.

"Emmett, will you kiss me again?"

"Whoa," he said to the horses as he pulled back on the reins. When he turned to her, he said, "I'll never say no to that, darlin'."

He pulled her close and put one hand on the back of her neck, while the other cradled her chin. He lowered his head and she stretched to meet him until their lips met. The butterflies inside her nearly took her breath, or was it Emmett doing that? His lips were soft, and the kiss was tender. Until it wasn't. His lips nipped at hers, loosely capturing her lower lip and pulling. He nipped again, teasing before he pressed more firmly. His lips were still soft, but they didn't seem as loose. They were now more insistent. She tried not to worry about kissing him the right or wrong way and just let him lead, following as though they were dancing. It seemed natural to part her mouth and let his tongue venture in. His touched hers and she felt the response deep inside her as a warmth that spread across her belly settled between her legs. Lacy thought she might have made a noise like a moan, but she wasn't sure. She wasn't sure of anything.

Emmett broke the kiss but pressed his forehead against hers instead of pulling away.

"I'm not totally sure, but I think that was a fine kiss," she said. "I felt it deep down inside me."

"It was a fine one, all right. It was a mighty fine one." He took her hand and put it on his hardness.

"Oh." It was not much more than a breathy whisper.

He kept her hand in his as he guided it along his length. His own fingers curled hers around it and held them there. "Darlin', I know you've never been kissed until today. How much do you know of sex?"

"I know what happens. I think I do, I mean, basically. And my mother had a talk with me on the train coming out here."

"She did? I've always heard it's hard for most mothers to do that. If you don't mind my asking, what did she tell you?"

Lacy didn't think there was any reason to keep from telling him. Maybe if he knew the extent of her understanding, he'd be able to make it better for her, to be more patient.

"I thought it was a nice talk. She told me not to be afraid to be playful. Well, she meant that about the relationship overall, to be playful and laugh together and you would probably like it if we're playful when we're intimate, too. The main thing she said was that when we are intimate, I should never say no to anything you want to do. She said there's a lot of pleasure in discovering new things, different... ways, she said. She told me about one or two friends she has who are unhappy and unful-filled. From what she learned about their relationships, their husbands just finally lost interest because they didn't show any interest."

That was a new one to Emmett. It had been his experience that mothers usually tell their daughters to endure it, that there wasn't much to enjoy for a woman. His opinion of Amelia went up a few notches.

"Why, does that sound right to you?" Lacy asked.

"She's a wise woman. It sounds like your mother wants the best for you and for you to enjoy our marriage to the fullest. I want you to enjoy our marriage to the fullest, too. I'll do my best to see that you do."

"I'll do my best, too, but Emmett, you may have to tell me how." Her voice was small.

"I think most of it will come naturally. Let's get on home now."

"Is it much farther?"

"Not really. Up ahead, you may be able to hear the river. There are some light rapids in a shallow part that runs parallel to this trail for a while. It's a pretty place."

"So you weren't kidding about that fishing spot, were you?"

He laughed. "No, I wasn't. Do you like to fish?"

"I've only been two or three times, but I had fun when I went."

"Good." He grinned at her. "The cabin's on the river. I built a dock I like to fish from sometimes."

"I'm eager to see it."

"We're close now. This trail goes right to it. It comes to a dead end at our house. I situated the cabin so that you don't see it from a long way off. The trail takes a good turn to the right, past the woods, and when you turn, there it is, straight ahead of you."

"It sounds nice."

"I fell in love with the location. It's a long ride to work every day, but I wouldn't want to move anywhere else."

"I hear the rapids now."

He beamed at her. "I love that sound. It means I'm almost home."

FOUR

Emmett rounded the bend, and the cabin came into view.

Lacy gasped. "Emmett! You never said it was this grand! When you said you built a cabin, I was expecting a small place. But this, this is a log mansion."

"I suppose you could call it that."

"You built this yourself?"

"Uncle Gann helped me. It took us a long time. I tried to make it with all the conveniences I've seen in other places."

"Does that mean we have running water? We didn't have running water until I was half grown."

"Hot and cold."

"We have hot running water?" Lacy asked, leaning forward, her eyes as wide as two full moons.

"Yes, ma'am, we do."

"Even in the water closet?"

"All three of them."

"No! We have three water closets? I never heard of such a thing. There are only two of us!"

"I call them bathrooms since they have tubs in them. And, yes, I built for future expansion."

"You plan to expand the house even more?"

"No, I plan to expand our family even more. I hope you want children."

"I do."

"Well, I built with a big family in mind."

"I can't believe what I'm seeing. I can't believe this is my home now."

He laughed again. "You haven't even seen the inside yet. You might not like it."

"Just look at all those chimneys. That's going to take a lot of wood."

"We don't have to heat all those rooms until some children come along."

"Then it'll take a lot of wood sometime in the future."

"I own a lot of land. We. *We* own a lot of land."

"I see the barn over there. Nice fence. Did you have to cut trees for that pasture or was it already open like that?"

"I had to cut a few."

"Emmett, I can hardly even think right now. This is all so much!"

"You'll get used to it soon. Right now, let's put your things on the porch. I'll come out later and take care of the team and put the wagon out by the barn."

He lifted her down again. Lacy reached for a bag, but he swatted her hand away. "I'll get those big ones. Here, you can take this. And this one. Now wait for me on the porch."

Emmett swatted her bottom as she started to walk away.

"Oh!" she said, startled, looking back at him.

"That was fun." He laughed to himself as he watched her walk away.

Hourglass figure, indeed.

SHE LOOKED at the front door, and it was so large that she felt dwarfed by it. The hardware made her think of castle doors she'd seen in fairy tale books. Although it was reminiscent of medieval times, it looked perfect against the huge logs of this home. It set an expectation that there were more grand things inside.

"You made these hinges and the door latch, didn't you? And the door knocker, too. I've never seen others like them."

"I did."

"Charlotte and Harriet were right. You are an artist. They're beautifully done."

"Thank you. Now close your eyes." She did, and she heard him open the door and suddenly she was swept up in his arms and carried across the threshold.

He set her down. "You may open them now."

Is this how Alice felt in Wonderland?

There was an offset foyer with hooks for coats and a full-length mirror on the wall to her right. She'd never seen a house with that; all the ones she'd seen opened directly into a parlor or sitting area, or maybe a small, boxy entryway. There was even a sturdy bench on the wall facing her. There was a metal art piece on the wall above the bench that depicted a forest. Each tree was individually crafted and welded to a large piece that represented the ground. "You made this?" she asked.

"I did," he said, pleased that she liked it. "I made the bench too."

"Emmett, you're incredibly talented." There was genuine awe in her voice.

"Thank you for saying so, but it's really just something I enjoy in my spare time."

She grinned at him. "I kind of like that you're modest about it, but this thing," she pointed to the wall art, "is museum quality."

He smiled at her in response and held out his hand. "Want to see the rest of the house?"

Lacy laughed. "I hope my heart can take the surprises."

"Well, let's find out."

He led her into a parlor she thought was huge. A massive rock fireplace dominated one end of it. A matching fireplace, only slightly smaller, took center stage at the other end of the room. The big one drew her eye, though. Lacy walked over to it and saw a metal arm anchored into the inside. It was in two folding parts held together so that the arm could be pulled out over the fire or put in place close to the inside wall. A huge pot, more like a cauldron, sat on the hearth.

"Does this arm hold the pot over the fire?"

"It does. I've used it a time or two for cooking, but only for the novelty of it. Except for when Gann comes over, I only cook for one. But I made a big ol' pot of stew that turned out pretty darned good."

Lacy walked around the room. There wasn't much furniture, but she supposed he didn't need much. She could already think of a few things she'd ask him to buy.

He took her through a dining area into the kitchen next, and Lacy immediately pictured herself rolling out pie crusts on the big work table. There was a big sink, and she ran to it to try out the hot water. It first came out tepid but quickly warmed up until it was hot. Emmett stood back and watched her and grinned when she laughed at it.

"How does the water get hot?" she asked.

"It's heated by fire and held in cisterns until you turn the tap. That activates a pump that brings it through the pipes. That's it in a nutshell, but there's a lot that goes into making it happen. It works great until I forget to add firewood," he admitted with a smile. "It still works, but the water isn't hot."

Emmett showed her the well-stocked pantry and a door

that opened to reveal steps down under the house to a cool cellar room. He opened the cabinets in the kitchen and showed her the dishes and cookware and kitchen items that had belonged to his mother. Lacy was thrilled with the assortment.

He took her next to the bathroom closest to the front of the house. She did the same thing with the hot water in the tub. She was even more impressed that the room had a small sink with hot and cold water rather than a pitcher and bowl that she was accustomed to. She stepped behind a walled partition and found the toilet. She peeked back around the partition at Emmett and said with delight, "It flushes."

He laughed.

"Let's go look at our room," he said.

"All right," she said and took the hand he offered.

He led her down a long hall, passing other rooms, through a door and she looked stunned. There was a large corner fireplace dominating one side of the room. The big bed on the other side of the room gave it balance. Heavy curtains were pulled to the sides of three large windows. Lacy had never seen windows that big that weren't in a storefront. The view of the river was breathtaking. She could see the dock he mentioned.

"I could look at this all day. You can see everything with these big windows," she said.

"It's nice to wake up to. And these are west-facing windows, so they catch the afternoon sun. It helps keep it warm in the winter. In the summer, those curtains keep out the heat."

She turned her attention to the bed. "You made this, too, didn't you?"

"I did," he answered.

It was a four-poster bed but had interesting metal work on the bottom half of the posts. Lacy touched the massive headboard and ran her fingers over it. It appeared to be hammered iron, with vertical spindle bars. The foot of the bed reflected the same style but wasn't as tall. The bed wasn't ornate, but it was striking. It had a rustic, solid, masculine feel.

There was a big dresser, a matching chest of drawers and a freestanding wardrobe. Emmett pointed out a door to a closet and she peeked in to see some of his clothing hanging on one side.

"I'll never have enough clothes for all this space," she said as she laughed.

"Maybe we should go on an extended honeymoon and I'll buy you more."

She started to tell him that sounded like fun, but she reconsidered. "A honeymoon would definitely be nice, but how many clothes do I really need in this town? I have enough now," she said with a chuckle.

"You aren't like other women, I don't think. Some would have jumped at the chance to go shopping for new clothes. Maybe most other women."

"We can compromise. You can take me on a honeymoon and buy me art supplies and fabrics to make things with."

"I would enjoy that, but I'll still buy you a few other things, too. So do you sew, or do you just prefer creating art pieces?"

"No, I sew, too. That's something you can buy for me—my own sewing machine. I used Mother's at home."

"Consider it done, darlin'."

She leaned against one of the posts at the foot of the bed, her arm around it in a lazy hug. "I like it when you call me *darlin'*."

Emmett flashed a grin that melted her a little bit. He walked over to her and pulled her into his arms. The kiss was possessive and powerful and left her a little weak. The thought struck her that it was an appropriate kiss to take place in a bedroom.

"Darlin'," Emmett said in a low voice. "I'll show you the rest of the house later. Right now, I think it's time we got this wedding dress off you."

She turned her back and let him unbutton it. When he finished the bottom button, she turned around. "Will you bring in my bags?"

"Of course." He went to get them and then set two of them on chairs and one on the dresser so she could open them and get to everything in them easily.

Lacy went to one and opened it. He glanced at the contents and saw a nightgown on top. It was flannel and had lace trim around the neck and button placket. The way it was folded concealed everything else under it.

Emmett sensed that Lacy was a little nervous. "I'll go on and move the wagon and take care of the horses. It shouldn't take too long."

"All right."

IT'S STILL LATE AFTERNOON. *Should I put on a gown this early? A different dress? Does the time make a difference? Probably not on a wedding night. Yes. I should definitely put on a gown. He wouldn't have said that about getting me out of my wedding dress if he wasn't ready to get intimate. Would he? Could he be getting hungry? Was that why he didn't want me in the dress, so I could whip up some supper without getting it dirty? No, no, not Emmett. He's not the kind of man to put off sexual relations. Surely not. I should put on that gown. Yes. That one.*

Lacy pulled out the skimpy gown from under the flannel. She took off her mother's wedding dress and found a hanger in the closet for it, then removed her petticoat and shift, folded them and found an empty dresser drawer to use. Her drawers fell to the floor and she picked them up and dropped them in a dirty clothes basket she'd seen in the closet earlier.

She looked in the freestanding mirror and saw her naked form. *Emmett will see me like this soon. I hope he's pleased.*

She slipped the soft nightie over her head and looked again in the mirror. It seemed like just a wisp of silky cotton. It had little cap sleeves that had more lace than fabric. The neckline was designed to rest loosely across the bosom, revealing a good bit of cleavage. It was cut on the bias and although it fell loosely and full, it hugged her curves as she moved. It came only inches below her bottom and had a narrow gathered flounce at the hem.

The material was thin and not exactly see-through, but she could just make out a hint of the dark triangle of her curls. She couldn't see the darker flesh of her nipples, but she couldn't hide the hard buds they'd become.

Lacy took the pins from her hair and grabbed her brush, raking it through the heavy waves to remove any tangles left from the bun.

She didn't hear Emmett approach the doorway, but when she heard him inhale sharply in a gasp, she turned to face him directly, her brush still in her right hand. She was standing in front of the windows, bathed in the late afternoon sun that revealed the outline of each of her curves through the fabric of the nightie.

"Lacy, darlin'," he said as he stepped into the room. He kicked off his boots and toed off his socks while he unbuttoned his shirt. "When I left the room, you were looking at a flannel nightgown. I'm sure it's a nice one, but I definitely like this one better."

"I'm glad you like it. I was afraid you might think it was too immodest or something."

Emmett laughed. "You're supposed to be immodest with

me. I dearly, fervently, earnestly, and intensely beg you to please be immodest with me."

Lacy's chuckle grew into a laugh.

He threw off the shirt and unfastened his britches. In no time, they were on the floor. He walked to her, took the brush from her hand and put it on the dresser. He lifted her chin so she'd look at him and lowered his face for a kiss.

When Emmett broke the kiss, he brought his hands up to her nipples, watching her face as he played with them. She stood still as he ran his thumbs over them, tweaked them, and lightly pinched them. He ran his fingernails back and forth over them. Her eyes closed, but her face still gave away her reactions to this new stimulation. He watched her lips form an O. He watched as she opened her mouth, and he watched as she took her lower lip between her teeth. When she began to sway on her feet, he kissed her again, pulling her hard against him. He kissed her mouth and then moved to her cheek and down to her neck.

Emmett ran his fingers through her hair and pulled it to make her angle her head. He concentrated on the sensitive point where neck meets shoulder and sucked it until the intensity made her pull away, but he held on to her and kept her from escaping.

"Emmett!"

He nuzzled her neck and whispered near her ear, "What is it, darlin'? Does that feel good?"

"Maybe too good. It's, um, too much."

"Where all did you feel it?" his gravelly voice asked as he continued to kiss her neck.

"I'm not sure—"

Emmett put a hand between her legs and cut off her words. "Did you feel it here?"

"Well, I—"

"You definitely felt it there. I can feel how wet you are. Give me your hand."

He didn't wait for her to offer her hand. He took it and put it between her legs. "Feel how wet you are, darlin'. You're wet for me." He took her hand and licked her juices from it, then he placed her hand on his hardness. "This is what you're doing to me."

She remembered her mother's advice about playfulness. "And that's a good thing, I take it?"

Emmett chuckled. "Yes, ma'am, it's definitely a good thing."

He ran his hands down her body, over her breasts, then at her sides where her waist nipped in and out again over her hips, then he brought them to rest at her waist. "Lacy, do you even know how perfect you are? This body, that face, I can hardly believe you're mine."

She smiled, happy that he was pleased with her. Her hands went up to his shoulders and she settled them on his chest, where she teased them through the black hairs there. "Maybe I'm the lucky one. You're a handsome man, you know. These muscles. Those eyes, and that smile." She ran her fingers over his lips. "I'm told you're quite the charmer. I hear women fall all over themselves getting to you."

"You may have heard exaggerations, darlin'. That sounds like Harriet talking. And I'm not too sure how she'd know that, since there aren't any single women in this town to be falling all over me."

They both laughed at that.

Emmett pulled her nightie over her head. "You can put this back on later if you want to, but now I have to see you. I need to touch you, all of you. Oh, sweet Lord, Lacy. Can I keep you naked all the time, I wonder?"

"Do you have enough wood for the fireplaces? I don't like being cold."

"If that's what it takes, I'll cut down every tree I own and everyone else's, too." He had her pulled to him and was running his hands all over her as he spoke. "Lacy, what a sweet, sweet ass this is," he said as he squeezed a cheek in each hand, glancing over her head at the mirror to see their reflection. "I want to kiss it, bite it, spank it, rub it, squeeze it, fuck it, and anything else I can think of."

"You want to spank it?" she asked, a little puzzled.

"Yes, ma'am, I do. I'll show you sometime." He looked at her and grinned and she knew he'd get everything he wanted from her. "Of all the things I mentioned, that's the only one that bothered you?"

"There was that other thing, you know, that word... did you mean"

"Yes, I did, darlin', but we can talk about all that later. Right now, though, I'm taking you to bed and making you mine."

"And kiss me more? I really like doing that."

"All over, darlin', I plan to kiss you all over."

FIVE

Later, Lacy lay next to Emmett with his arm under her neck.

"Do you feel any different?" he asked.

"You mean do I feel like a woman now? A properly married woman? Or are you asking if I think I'll survive having my tender little tunnel assaulted by your giant sequoia?"

He burst out laughing. "Why, darlin', you flatter me. I know I'm not a giant sequoia. A majestic pine, maybe. No, let's go with oak. It's a hardwood. I'm a mighty oak. Did my mighty oak hurt your little tunnel?"

"No, not really. It could use a nice, hot soak, though. Do you mind if I bathe?"

"It's a big tub. We can bathe together."

She smiled. "I saw how big our tub is. I was kind of hoping we could. I never bathed with anyone else before."

"So, two brand new experiences in one day. Fucking and bathing with a man."

"More than that! Let's see, there's that word you said, and bathing with a man, and getting married, and seeing a naked man. Does touching a naked man count as another first?"

"It certainly ought to. Getting married was a first for me,

too. Seeing you naked was a first. That and fucking you are the best ones, of course. Having a mother-in-law—do you think that counts as a first?"

"It should. Another first for me is having a home with hot running water. And we both just met each other today, so we both get firsts for that."

Emmett thought about the firsts and how little time had actually passed since Harriet and Mrs. Copperfield had come to see him in his shop that day. "I'm awfully glad that what just happened, you know, happened. A couple of people warned me not to pressure you into the physical side of marriage too soon, and I understood what they meant. Some women might not feel comfortable doing that with someone they just met, even if they are married. It might be too hard to give yourself to a stranger."

Emmett felt her smile against the side of his chest before she spoke. "Mother and I had a talk about that on the train because I wondered about it, too. Since you wanted to marry me sight unseen immediately, we had a feeling you're a man of action, so to speak, a man who might not be willing to put things off. I didn't want to disappoint you on our wedding night. Besides, I wouldn't be comfortable being husband and wife in name only. If I'm going to be married, I want the whole thing." She turned to look at him. "You already married me, so I guess it's safe to tell you that when I first saw you, I was smitten. Then when you kissed me, well, I would have been fine doing it there in the road."

Emmett laughed softly and turned, putting his arm around her. "Then it's safe to tell you I was smitten when I first saw you, too. I couldn't believe how lucky I was to get a woman like you for a wife. Tell me something, do you feel like an old married lady yet?"

"Not an old one, just an achy one," she said.

"Are you hungry? I am. Want to bathe first or eat first?"

"Eat first. I like to take my time in a bath and have a good soak."

"All right, that sounds perfect. There's plenty of food so we don't need to cook. We can just heat up something." He stood up. "Come on."

"Wait a minute," she said as she took his hand, "we need to put something on."

"No, we don't. There's nobody here but us and we'll just have to take our clothes off again to bathe."

She shrugged her shoulders. "I can't find a flaw in that logic."

He smirked. "I'm not ashamed to tell you I spent some time thinking of how I could keep you naked. I thought it was a well-reasoned argument."

She grinned at him. "Don't you love it when you can execute a good plan successfully?"

CHARLOTTE BROUGHT Amelia another cup of tea then sat down beside her on the porch swing.

"I can't tell you how happy I am that we could find a husband for Lacy and get her out of that situation in Laramie. I've seen how narrow-minded people can ruin someone's life," Charlotte said.

"Some of them are not just narrow-minded, they're closed-minded people, simply unwilling to listen to anyone whose viewpoint differs from theirs. I thought they were our friends. Most of them know Lacy enough to know the rumors couldn't be true," Amelia said. "I don't even want to repeat some of the vicious things they said about my baby."

"I can imagine. The good thing is that I do believe Emmett is a good man."

Amelia smiled. "He certainly is an attractive one."

"Yes, he is definitely that," Charlotte said with a giggle. "Let's be happy it worked out for her so well in that regard. As beautiful as she is, I like to think they might have found each other anyway. I mean, if the world were a fair place."

"It isn't, though. Even Lacy doesn't know all of the distasteful things that went on back in Laramie. Carl, the young man who was murdered, had a brother named Gerald. A bad sort. He went to see George and made an offer to marry Lacy after Carl's death. He said he wanted to 'help her save face' after what Carl did to her. George told him he would not give his blessing or even his permission for their union. He told him he didn't believe Carl did anything untoward to Lacy. Gerald didn't take it well. He blew up and threatened to hurt our family. Gerald's always had a reputation for being unstable and volatile. I shudder to think what might have happened if we hadn't gotten Lacy out of town quickly. I just hope she's far enough away here to be removed from the unpleasantness."

"If you think Gerald might come here and cause a problem, I daresay Emmett can take care of the man in a trice."

"Yes," Amelia smiled, "it does seem that blacksmithing is keeping him in fine fighting form."

"Am, I still don't understand how they could suspect Lacy of murder in the first place. She was waiting with you for the ceremony to start, wasn't she? Don't they have any other suspects?"

"She was with me all morning, but Deputy Faust insists she could have had an accomplice, or she could have slipped away since they lived so close. Of course, he hasn't mentioned who that accomplice could possibly be. I don't know if the law suspects anyone else; they're pretty tight-lipped about it. But

George and I have come up with some other names. Gerald, for one. Their parents were well-off and sick. With Carl gone, he would inherit everything."

"That sounds like a good motive if there was a lot of money."

"I'm not sure, but we believe it's a lot. And then there's Alan Huntsman, Carl's friend. Lacy said they were always together when she was with Carl. We didn't think anything about it until after the murder when Lacy told us more about him. There just seems to be something odd about the man. George wonders if there isn't something, well, unusual about the relationship. You know, between the two men."

"Oh, my."

"We didn't tell Lacy about George's suspicions. There really wasn't any point since Carl was dead. The other person we considered, or the other two people, were Heather Matthews and her brother Harold. Apparently, Carl was keeping company with Heather during the time he was seeing Lacy. Now I don't believe the girl is capable of it, but George says he believes jealousy can make people act irrationally. He believes anyone's capable of it. And then there's Harold. He could have killed him for Heather's honor, if he believed Carl molested her. Those are the ones we can think of, and to our knowledge, they haven't been investigated."

"Why on earth not? Surely, they know about them."

"Deputy Elwin Faust is the primary person working on the murder," Amelia said with a sigh. "Last year, he came to George to ask for permission to court Lacy. We don't particularly care for him; he's a little weasel of a man. Of course, he said no. George never even mentioned it to her. Our speculation is that he'd love to take down our family a peg. I don't think he'd mind hurting Lacy at all."

"Oh, Am, there's just so much to have to deal with. It must

be an awful burden for you and George. I can see that you're holding up; tell me how George is doing."

"Since that sickness he had, he's been weak. We've tried to protect Lacy from that, too. He gets pained and tired easily. He's not the man he was, Charlotte. This situation with Lacy has taken its toll on what good health he had."

"Well, now that it's resolved, maybe he can start getting some rest."

"That's a nice thought, but I don't think he'll rest easy until someone's convicted of murder and that someone's not Lacy."

"Would you like some more dessert?"

"No, thank you. It just hit me how tired I am after that trip and the excitement of the wedding today. If it's all right with you, I think I'll go ahead and retire."

"Oh, of course, I should have realized how worn out you'd be." Charlotte paused. "It sure is good to have you here, Amelia."

LACY TURNED on the hot water in the bathtub and smiled as it turned hot with her hand under the hot water spigot. It got too hot, so she had to turn the cold water tap on, too. It had a separate spigot, so she had to bend over and dip her hand in the water to feel how hot the bathwater was, and she adjusted the knobs accordingly.

Emmett walked in and saw her bent over the bathtub. "Oh, Lacy girl, this view I have right now..."

She started to get up, but he was quick enough to put his hand on her back and keep her there. "Let me enjoy this." She felt awfully exposed, but his request seemed within his rights as her husband.

Emmett straddled her bottom and legs and bent over so he

could reach her breasts. "I love playing with these, you know. I love how they feel, how they move, how these nips get hard and how it makes you get excited when I suck on them. *Damn*. I was going to wait until after our bath before I fucked you again, but I don't think I want to wait."

"We can always do it again after our bath," Lacy said suggestively.

She could hear the smile in his voice when he said, "Yes, we can. Right now, though, we're going to do this." He looked around and pulled over a small, padded stool. "Put your knees on this, I need you raised up a little bit."

Lacy did and found that her bottom was raised quite a bit, almost embarrassingly so. Her hands were still on the bottom of the tub.

Emmett put his hand between her legs. "So wet already, darlin'. I'm going to fuck you right here," he said as he put two fingers up inside her and slowly thrust them in and out. "Now this position lends itself to me fucking you right here, too." He withdrew his wet fingers and circled her little brown rosette. She gasped and turned her head sharply, and he chuckled, quickly inserting one finger just inside before she knew what was happening. "You're so tight. That'll feel like Heaven to my cock. But not tonight." He withdrew his finger and slapped her bottom. "I guess I don't have to tell you this position also lends itself to me spanking you, too." He swatted her again.

"You'll do that to me?"

He chuckled. "You mean fuck your ass or spank it?"

"Well," she began.

"Doesn't matter. It's yes to both."

"Are you talking about a spanking as in being playful with me?"

"Absolutely. I like playfulness. Your mother gave you good advice. It can be really, uh, exciting. For both of us."

He swatted her bottom playfully again and she wagged it. So he swatted it again. Then Emmett put his hand between her legs again and found her even wetter. He noticed the level of water in the tub and reached over to turn off the taps.

He put his fingers inside her again, pumping at a good, quick pace. Lacy moaned.

"Tell me, darlin', are you afraid I'll give you a real spanking sometime?"

He quickened his pace, and she moaned a little more insistently.

"Answer me. Were you afraid I'll punish you with a spanking?"

"Uhm," was her muffled response.

"I can't understand you, babe. Do you want to know if I'll ever spank you for your behavior?"

Her breath was coming faster, as were his fingers inside her. She pushed back against them with each thrust and Emmett thought he could watch her breasts bounce around like that forever. He hoped he could dream about them moving like that.

"Hmm. Yes," she managed to say as she struggled with her words.

"I believe I might. I probably would if I thought you needed it."

She made a sound of whimpering protest.

"You don't think you'd like for me to spank you?" His fingers moved faster and harder.

"Uhm, nhh, no," she said. Her breathing was labored.

His free hand grabbed one buttock and squeezed it. "If you act up, if you disobey me, if you get yourself in danger out here, if I think you deserve it, I'm going to paint this ass as red as the sun, and almost as hot. Don't you think I should?"

He inserted a third finger up into her wetness while he

plunged his thumb into her other hole. Lacy threw back her head in protest but didn't skip a beat at meeting his thrusts. That both amused him and nearly sent his seed flying.

"Are you ready for me, darlin'?"

"Yes!"

"I want to hear more." His hands continued to torment her.

"Uh. Uh. What?" Her words were barely intelligible.

"I want you to beg me to spank you when you're bad."

"No." It was faint, but he heard it.

His fingers moved to her little swollen bud. The writhing of her body told him his fingers were having the desired effect.

He leaned over nearer her ear and said it softly. "Say it. Beg me."

He heard only her fast breathing.

His fingers increased pressure on her bud. "Say it."

He withdrew his hands completely.

"No! Please, don't stop."

"Beg me to spank you."

Lacy took a couple of deep, fast breaths. "Please spank me when I'm bad!" It was almost a shout.

Emmett plunged inside her and thrust fast and hard. His hands held her below her tiny waist at her hips. When she pushed back, he helped by pulling her body hard against him.

Her cries of need were the sweetest of sounds to his ears and he gave her what she needed until both of them spent and fell to the floor. They stayed there until their heartbeats calmed and their breaths normalized.

"Sure is a good thing we have hot running water," she said. "I bet our bath is cold by now."

LATER THAT NIGHT as they lay in bed together, Lacy asked the question that had bothered her since just before their bath.

"All that talk about spanking me for real, that was just the, um, excitement of the moment, wasn't it? You wouldn't really do that, right?

Emmett grinned and looked down at her, raising one eyebrow. He didn't answer.

SIX

The next morning, Emmett and Lacy stayed in bed much longer than either of them normally would have. Both of them knew it was because they'd awakened twice in the night to make love, although neither of them called it that. Emmett called it *fucking* and Lacy called it *that word you said*.

After enjoying their bodies one last, leisurely time, they rose for breakfast and again ate in the nude. Lacy invited him to take another bath with her, and he agreed, but he wanted to go tend to the animals first. She cleaned the breakfast mess while he went out, naked.

"MAKE a list of things you want from the mercantile and we'll stop there before we pick up your mother. I know you mentioned something, and I forgot what it was already."

Lacy smiled. "Mother always said that was part of being a man. Father didn't have a mind for remembering those little things, either. I think it was scented bath oils. It would be nice to put them in Mother's room, too."

"I hope she likes the house."

"Honey, she may love it even more than I do, if it's possible. That hot water alone is going to make her green with envy."

"There's a reason it's not so common out here. It's expensive and tedious as hell to get it set up. Back east, they mostly use coal to heat the water, but out here, there aren't any coal mines so there's nobody to deliver a wagonload of coal whenever we run out. I did make it where we could use coal, though, and oil, too, in the future. But for now, we're stuck with wood. Good thing we have lots of it."

"You must do an awful lot of wood chopping."

He flexed his arm. "Feel these muscles."

She did. "Those muscles were the second thing I noticed about you that made me want you."

"Stop talking like that, darlin', or we'll be late getting your mother. Here's some paper and a pencil. Put down eggs. And butter."

"Emmett?"

"Yes'm?"

"I'm a city girl, you know, and I always wished we lived where we could have chickens and fresh eggs. Will you let me have chickens?"

"Of course, darlin'. You can even help me build a coop and put up a fence. That'll be fun."

"It will be!"

"It'll cost you, of course," he said with a grin.

"It will, huh? So, will I be paying you on my knees or astride the mighty oak?"

Emmett beamed at her. "I may have thought up something else by then."

"Well, I do want a chicken coop," she said with a sigh.

He chuckled. "Oh, let's get some tea, too. We've been drinking it more than I usually do. How about jelly? They usually have some that's been made by women in town. Want to stop at Mary's and get a pie on the way home? I've done it before. We have to take the pie pan back to her, though. Milk. We'll see if they've got fresh milk left. I'm probably going to want cream with that pie."

She wrote it all down. "I can make you a pie. I'm pretty good at it."

"Good. But I don't want you to spend your time on drudgery while your mother's visiting."

"She loves to cook and bake, Emmett. When she sees that kitchen, we might not be able to keep her out."

He threw up his hands and laughed. "Whatever it takes to make you two happy."

"She's going to be blown away when she learns I'm a rich woman now. She never doubted you could support me as a blacksmith, but when she sees this and finds out about the silver mine, she won't know how to react."

"I hope she'll be pleased." He paused. "You know, Lacy, since I married you, your mother and father are my family now, too. I promise you they'll never lack for money if misfortune comes along. I'll take care of them."

She stood and threw her arms around him, her eyes welling up. "Oh, Emmett, I love you so much."

He held her so tight, she was on the verge of having difficulty breathing.

"Lacy, darlin', you don't know how it makes me feel to hear those words from you. I love you, too. I haven't said it yet because I didn't want you to feel pressured into saying it back if you don't feel that way yet. But I do. I think I loved you from the first time I saw you."

A few tears fell from her eyes before she pulled away. "Well, now that that's settled, I need to finish the grocery list." She wiped her tears on her apron.

Emmett smiled at her. His heart was smiling, too.

The ride to the mercantile was quiet. They held hands or had a hand on the other's leg, or his arm was around her. One way or another, they were touching the whole way. He pointed out a trail that was even less traveled than the one they were on and said it was another good way to get to his Uncle Gann's house. She hadn't even noticed it the day when he first brought her. He told her another trail that started down by the river behind their house met up with this trail in the woods. The other way was to go all the way through town and past the old silver mine, but this path was more direct.

"When do I get to meet this Uncle Gann?"

"Anytime you want to, I expect. He usually comes around every two or three days unless we're working on something. He's probably staying away to give us privacy. We could wait for him to come by, or we could even take your mother with us and go for a visit. She might appreciate meeting my whole family, such as it is."

"What would Uncle Gann think about us just dropping in?"

"He'd probably like it. He's up for anything. You'll like him."

"Does he have a big house, too?"

"It's not quite as big, but it's still impressive. It's the house my granddad built, the house Gann and my mother grew up in. Obviously, it's an older place. It's a log house, too. Our current project is to get hot running water for his house. We've already got all the supplies; we just need to get together and do it."

"Oh, I feel bad about hampering your progress on his house. You stopped because of me, didn't you?"

"I stopped because I got married. And don't ask me if I'd rather be sweating over a heavy construction job at his house or be at home fucking my wife. I think you already know the answer to that."

She smiled. "I know which one I'd choose."

The conversation continued all the way to the mercantile. It was at times innocent, suggestive, or downright dirty and sexy.

Emmett set the brake on the wagon, jumped down, and lifted his wife to the ground. Shirley greeted them when they entered.

"Good afternoon, Emmett, and you must be Lacy. Welcome to Big Rock, dear. I'm Shirley Keller, a member of the Ladies' Aid Society. We're the ones who run the mail order bride operation. I'm just tickled pink we were able to find a match for you. You both look like we did a good job, I must say."

"It's nice to meet you, Shirley. Yes, I believe your group did a wonderful job when you thought to introduce us."

"We may just be the best match you've made yet, Shirley," Emmett said with a big smile.

"Now Lacy, we'd love for you to join our Society. We meet once a month, usually every third Thursday. We meet at the community hall. I hope you'll at least visit and consider joining us."

"I will visit. Thank you for inviting me."

"Well, don't let me keep you two from shopping. You're probably eager to be on your way." She returned to her place behind the counter, working on a ledger.

Emmett picked up a big basket to collect items and started to lead her around the store. The first thing he did was pick up a big box of eggs and took them to Shirley at the desk. "I want the whole box, but we aren't through yet."

"I'll guard them with my life, Emmett," she said with her dry wit.

He caught back up with Lacy and held out the basket for the two pint jars of jelly she had in her hand. He looked back up at Shirley at the desk. "Shirley, do you have a couple of pounds of butter and some milk? I didn't bring a milk jar to refill; we're not quite out yet."

"I do. I'll get it for you. You can just bring this jar back next time you're in."

"Thank you, ma'am," he said cheerfully.

"Here's the tea," Lacy said to Emmett. "How much of it do you think we should get?"

"Let's get the whole tin." He picked it up and put it in the basket, where it took up a good bit of space.

She shook her head in wonder. "I've never seen anyone buy the whole thing before. Most people just get small amounts, you know."

"Most people don't know how to live."

She shook her head again, but this time she was smiling. She came to the soaps and toiletries and Emmett would have sworn she picked up every bottle and bar to smell. Lacy selected some scented bath oils and pretty milled soaps for their baths.

"If you're going to smell that good, I may not be able to keep away from you."

"You already can't keep away from me."

"Don't get sassy with me, darlin'. I just might use this on you." He picked up a big wooden spoon from a crockery jar.

"Emmett!" It was a whisper. "Someone might hear."

"They will when I start swinging this baby." He made a motion akin to swinging it like a paddle. "Wow. It's got some heft." He looked at her with that eyebrow raised, a smirk, and a gleam in his eye. "You might not like this too much. It'll turn that sweet ass red and hot in no time at all."

"Emmett, please!" The whispered words implored him not to talk loud enough to embarrass her.

The smirk grew into a grin and he slipped the spoon into their basket.

They picked up a few more items, several they didn't really need but Emmett wanted. Lacy was quiet as they checked out and he loaded the wagon.

Once underway again, she had to ask. "Do you really plan to use that spoon to spank me?"

Once again, he grinned at her but didn't answer. He did put his arm around her, though.

LACY SAT between Amelia and Emmett on the wagon seat. That uneasy feeling Emmett gave her when the subject of spanking came up was gone. She was eager for her mother to see her new home. She knew her mother would have the same reaction to the house she had had.

"Emmett," Amelia said, "I do appreciate it that you invited me to spend some more time with Lacy, and with you, too, before I have to leave to go home. It's going to be awfully lonely at home without her."

"I meant it when I said you're welcome to come anytime and stay as long as you want. The only family I've had for years now is my Uncle Gann. It's nice to expand that circle a little bit."

"Those are sweet words to hear, Emmett. I'm so happy with the way everything turned out with you two. Of course, I'm basing that on how happy you both look. Please tell me you're both happy with this outcome, too."

"Is it all right if I call you Amelia?"

"Yes, please!"

"Well, Amelia, I think it's safe to say we're both ecstatic. I've never in my life been this happy, and I'm a pretty content guy overall."

Lacy looked at her mother with a conspiratorial satisfaction, and with a little mischief peeking out under her lashes. Amelia understood immediately and looked down to keep from giggling.

"I'm so thrilled to hear that. George will be, too," she said with an almost completely straight face.

"Mother, there is something you need to know about Emmett before we get to the house. It's something that took me completely by surprise. Something that Miz Charlotte probably doesn't even know."

"Oh, dear, this sounds serious. What is it, Lacy? Is there a problem?"

"No, no problem at all. As a matter of fact, it's a wonderful thing. It was just a surprise to me when Emmett told me; I thought he might be joking. Then when I saw the cabin, I believed him."

Amelia's eyes went from Lacy to Emmett's smiling face and back.

"Well, you may not know that Big Rock originally had a silver mine a few years back. It's depleted now, but it was quite productive in its heyday," Lacy explained.

"I have heard that, now that you mention it. I had forgotten."

"The man who discovered the ore, who owned the mine, was Emmett's grandfather. Emmett's mother and his uncle inherited when the grandfather died. Of course, Emmett inherited when his mother passed away. Emmett's a rich man, Mother. Very rich."

"*We're* rich, darlin'. We're married now," he said.

"Is this true?" Amelia asked.

"Yes, ma'am, it is," Emmett said.

"B-but you're a blacksmith."

He smiled. "I sure am. My father taught me how to work with metals and I enjoy it. I work because I want to."

"I don't know what to say, besides maybe *thank you, Lord*. We always prayed you'd find a man who could take care of you. He answered that one, all right!"

"You're going to love the house, Mother. It's almost unbelievable."

"Oh, I can hardly wait to see it now," Amelia said.

Lacy asked Emmett to tell her mother about how he had made their wedding bands and the story behind them. Amelia thought it said much about Emmett's character that he wanted to go to that much trouble for his wife. She was growing to appreciate the man more by the minute.

When they got closer to the house, Lacy pointed out the trail to Gann's house. "We plan to go visit him while you're here. He's the only family Emmett has, and he wants us both to meet him."

"All right, if you don't think he'd mind us dropping by."

Emmett chuckled. "That's how we are out here. We don't stand on ceremony like waiting for invitations, especially when it's with family. Gann's a good man. I think you'll both like him."

"The house is just up around this bend up here," Lacy said, nodding her head in that direction.

When they rounded the corner and she saw the house, Amelia's reaction was much like Lacy's was. "Oh, my," she said with wonder. "And there's the river; what a lovely backdrop. Oh, that's your fishing spot, isn't it?" she asked.

"There are two or three places where the fishing's almost always good. I plan to make a diehard fisherwoman out of your daughter."

When Emmett brought the wagon to a stop in front of the porch steps, he told Lacy to take her mother on in while he got the bags and supplies.

Amelia commented on the huge door, first thing.

"Emmett made the door hardware; it's one-of-a-kind."

When they went inside, Amelia was impressed with the metal wall sculpture Emmett had made. "That's just beautiful. Those trees have so much detail."

The rest of the house impressed her just as much. Amelia had never seen a room in a private home that had two fireplaces in it. She'd certainly never seen a private home with three water closets. As Lacy suspected, the hot running water was deemed her favorite feature.

She showed her mother to the room Emmett had prepared for her. It was larger than the other bedrooms and had its own water closet attached. Amelia was most appreciative.

In the kitchen, Amelia *oohed* and *aahed* as she pulled all the doors, drawers and cabinets open, to see what was inside. It made her want to cook, just as Lacy said it would. They checked all the food and decided what to make for supper.

Emmett brought in her bags and put them in her room. The last things he brought in were the bags from the mercantile and the pie from Mary's restaurant. All three of them helped put up the kitchen supplies. He surreptitiously winked at his wife when he put the wooden spoon away. Lacy handed one bottle of bath oil and a packet of sweet-smelling soap to her mother and took the other ones to her bath. While they were putting those things in the proper place, he put on a kettle of water to make a pot of tea.

While the three sat at the table with their tea, Emmett mentioned a honeymoon. "You know, darlin', we never did talk about where you'd like to go. I'll take you anywhere."

"I've thought about it, and wherever we go, I'd like to start in Laramie. I want you to meet Father and I know he wants to meet you, too. He really wanted to be here."

"Good idea, I want to meet him, too. Then maybe on to Cheyenne? I can show you where I was born and lived as a child. Besides, it's a bigger city and I can buy you more things."

"Emmett," she grinned at him, "I don't need a lot of things."

"I know, I know, but you have to let me get you a few things. I want to."

"All right. You win." She threw her hands up in defeat.

"Why don't we go on over and let me introduce you to Gann?"

"It'll be lunchtime before too long," Amelia said. "I wouldn't feel right barging in on him at mealtime. Would it be all right if we pack up food for all of us and take that pie?"

"Great idea," Emmett said as he downed the last of his tea and jumped up. "I'll go get a couple of boxes while you two decide what you want to take."

They were on the road in no time. Emmett was glad he hadn't immediately unhooked the horses when they got home.

"Tell us about your uncle, Emmett," Amelia said.

"All right. He was my mother's baby brother, and I'm told she stopped picking on him as soon as he got taller than she was. She adored him, though. It was mutual. When she married Dad, Gann was still a kid. That didn't stop him from telling my dad that if he mistreated my mother, he'd have to answer to him. Dad could have laughed it off, but he said he could see how much Gann loved Mom. He promised to treat her well and vowed that Gann would never have a reason to doubt him. They shook hands like two grownup men." Emmett warmed to the memory. "I heard Dad tell that story several times, and he always said it in deference to how much he respected Gann for that."

"That's so sweet, Emmett," Lacy said.

"It is, isn't it? He took it real hard when Mom passed, just as hard as Dad and I did. He disappeared for a few days. To this day, we don't know where he went, and he doesn't talk about it."

"You told me he's not married. How old is he?"

"Thirty-nine."

"Oh, he's young still. He's just a year older than Mother."

"Now you don't have to go blabbing my age to everybody, Lacy. A woman has to have her mystery, you know."

"Hogwash. You should be proud. You could still pass for thirty, Mother."

Amelia waved off the comment. "Now that's hogwash, dear. Pure drivel."

"No, it's not, Amelia," Emmett offered. "It's clear where Lacy gets her beauty."

Lacy saw the blush on her mother's cheeks. Thirty-eight years old, and she blushed. Lacy was reminded of what her mother said about George not being able to perform as a man anymore. Her heart went out to her mother.

"The house isn't far now; you'll see it in just a little bit. It's an older cabin, but it's still pretty impressive. Granddad built a small cabin when he first started out, then as his wealth grew, he built the house you'll see. The original cabin is still out back. Gann uses it as a workshop and woodshed."

They saw the barn and the original cabin before they saw the house, since the trail from Emmett's house was behind it. When they drove around to the front, the ladies became more excited to see it and the inside, too. Emmett helped them down and they all three walked up the wide steps together. Emmett knocked on the door.

Gann Douglas wasn't what Lacy had expected, or Amelia, either, for that matter. He was as tall as Emmett. They might have been brothers.

Gann broke out in a big smile when he saw Emmett. "I was wondering when I'd get to meet your wife." He looked at the two women. "Which one is she?"

The ladies were immediately at ease with him and appreciated his humor. "That would be me; I'm Lacy. This is my mother, Amelia."

"Come on in. I can't tell you what a pleasure it is to meet you. Emmett, you are a lucky man."

"Yes, I am, no doubt about it."

"Gann, we brought lunch. If you'll point us to the kitchen, Mother and I can be getting it ready while you and Emmett chat."

"Oh, heavens, no, I don't think so. I'd rather spend my time with the pretty ladies than with him. Kitchen's this way. Let's see what you brought. Emmett, you can stay in here or come sit at the table. Your choice." He spoke the last sentences as he led them through the parlor.

"All right, the pantry's behind that door. Silverware's in that drawer, and let me get out plates and glasses. What are we having? Should I light the stove?"

"We didn't really cook. Emmett wanted to come on the spur of the moment. We have a loaf and a half of bread, butter, jelly, cheeses, apples, and cold roast slices. And a pie from Mary's."

"Sounds like a feast to me. There's my good bread knife over there. Hand me that, would you?"

Emmett handed it to him.

"I have some applesauce that would be great on some fried bread. Emmett, light that stove, will you? And while we're at it, let's take another pan and fry up some buttery beef and cheese sandwiches. Let me go get my butter. I use a lot of it!"

He walked out the door and into the cellar to get the butter and applesauce. He picked up milk and cream, too. He tucked a wrapped wedge of cheddar in the waist of his britches since his hands were full.

Lacy looked at Emmett. "I see what you mean," she said.

He chuckled. "That's nothing."

Emmett got the fire going hot enough to heat the skillets.

They set up an assembly line of sorts, one buttering bread, another frying it in more butter on both sides, another assembling the sliced cheese and roast beef between two slices of buttered bread.

"This can be our appetizer. Toast and applesauce and toast and jelly." He slapped the hot bread on plates and put them on the table. "It'll take a few minutes for the sandwiches to get hot enough to melt the cheese. Let's offer thanks and dig in."

They took their seats and Gann asked the blessing. Emmett glanced at Lacy when the prayer was over, a little embarrassed that he hadn't thought to pray before their meals since they'd been married. He would have to remedy that.

"Gann, this applesauce is delicious," Lacy said. "Did you make it or buy it?"

"You said that like you don't believe I can cook," he said. His smile belied the words. "I did, I made it all by myself. Here, have some more."

"Did you take up the family business in any way?" Amelia asked, just to make conversation. "Emmett's father taught him smithing, and apparently, he knows how to work with ores. Did you follow that path?"

"I dabbled in the metallurgy side of it, but what I really enjoyed was construction. Then when I inherited money, I bought a few old buildings in Rawlins and fixed them up. I even had a couple of new ones built, too. Turned them all into business office units or apartments and I rent them out. I have a property manager to take care of all the hassles, so I sit back and get rent money every month."

"Oh, I see now how you were able to help Emmett so much on the house. That seems like a very smart business enterprise," Lacy said.

"It is. Before I inherited, shoot, before I even realized I would inherit anything, I saw men who worked at the mine for years and then either just got too old or were injured and unable to work. Suddenly, they had no income, no way to take care of their wives or families. Dad helped them out and gave them food and money, but they hated to accept it. It was humbling to them, even shameful in their eyes, to have to accept his help. To Dad, they were his friends and he wanted to help. I decided to figure out a way to always have an income even if I couldn't work. I knew I had to get into real estate for that; it was the only thing I could think of."

"I can appreciate that more than you know," Amelia said. "We have a store in Laramie. George, that's my husband, got sick two years ago and his health isn't what you'd expect for a man his age. He's still working, but it's harder and harder on him as weeks and months go by. We don't have any other income like you mention, so we've saved as much as we could. We always did, but we've recently become more diligent in doing so." She gave a rueful half-shrug. "You know that expression that says you have everything if you have your health? There's truth to it. It's a very stark reality that hits you when suddenly your health isn't what it was."

"Do you own the store outright?" Gann asked.

"Yes," Amelia replied.

"Then you can do what I described. You can make an arrangement where someone else runs the store and you get a percentage of sales. Or you could keep the building and sell the goods to someone who wants his own store. He'll have the store himself, but you could still charge rent for the building."

"Why, you're right. For some reason, the only avenue I ever considered was selling the entire store, building and all."

Gann smiled. "There are arguments for that, too. Let's say you wanted to move here and be close to Lacy and all those future grandbabies. You might not want to be an absentee landlord even if you do have a property manager doing the work. Some owners like to be able to stay close to their properties."

Amelia laughed a little bit. "This little luncheon has been invaluable for me. If George's health continues to decline, I may be faced with unpleasant decisions in the future. If that should happen and I need advice, would it be all right if I come to you for guidance?"

Gann's face softened then reflected a grin. "I hope you do come to me. I mean, we're almost sort of family now. That's what almost sort of families do, they help each other."

Gann got up and took the hot sandwiches out of the pan. He sliced each one diagonally and served them.

"How long do you plan to visit, Amelia?" Gann asked.

"I'll catch the stage Monday. That'll get me home Thursday. I really need to check on George. I'd like to have stayed longer."

"Could you wire him and ask how he's holding up? If he seems to be doing well, perhaps you could stay a few extra days."

"I think I should go. I'll try to come back soon. And often," she added. "Emmett, do you attend church?"

Gann broke out in a big laugh.

Emmett gave him a stern look. "Not every week, but I go more often than I don't."

"His mother would tear him up for not going regularly," Gann said.

"I didn't mean to start anything between you two," she chuckled, "but I'd really like to go and hear Willis preach again. They're such dear friends of ours."

"I'd be happy to take you both to church tomorrow," Emmett said.

Gann sliced the blackberry pie and put a big piece in front of everyone. He put a little pitcher of cream in the middle of the table. As they dug in, the conversation again turned to a honeymoon.

"Didn't you tell me you wanted to take Lacy on a honeymoon trip as soon as you got the chance?" he asked.

"I did," Emmett replied after he swallowed a big bite. "We're going to start out in Laramie for a few days, so I can meet Lacy's father. Then we might go on to Cheyenne and stay for a while, then come back and stop in Laramie again. I don't have any idea how long we'll stay in either place or when we'll get back. What do you think, Lacy? If we leave here Friday, we can be in Laramie on Monday."

"All right, that sounds fine. It sounds quick, but fine."

"That sounds like a good trip," Gann said. "Just let me know so I can take care of your animals."

"That reminds me," Emmett said. "Lacy wants to get chickens."

"Wonderful!" Gann said. "I saw a chicken coop in Rawlins like you wouldn't believe. It was more like a chicken palace," he said as he grabbed a piece of paper from the sideboard behind him and pulled a stubby pencil from his pocket and started drawing plans.

"SO, do you think your mother retired early because she was tired or because she wanted to give us newlywed time?" Emmett asked as he took off his shirt.

"Well, she did look tired, but after that talk on the train, maybe she wanted to do her part and give us another chance to take her advice."

"I like your mother, and not because of that. Well, I do like her because of that, but not just because of that."

"I love her too, but it sure seems odd to do... this," she waved toward the bed, "with her in the house. What if she hears us?"

"Then she'll know you're taking her advice."

"It would be embarrassing."

Emmett got a look of pure mischief, of downright evil, on his face. "Do you think so?"

"Yes. I think I'll wear the flannel nightgown."

"Is it your time of the month?"

"No."

"Is there snow on the ground?"

"No."

"Then please, no flannel, darlin'. Any of those others will do nicely, though."

She saw his grin and the fact that he was naked already and knew he wouldn't just let her go to sleep. She reached in her drawer and pulled out one of the less sheer nighties and headed to their bathroom to ready herself for bed—and for him.

When she walked out of the bathroom, she found him lying stretched out on his back on the bed, arms behind his head, legs comfortably crossed, with his hard length looking like it was trying to reach the ceiling. Lacy loved to see him like this, all those delicious muscles bulging, his desire obvious, and that look in his eyes that made her know she was his.

"The mighty oak has grown already," she said.

"All I have to do is think about you and it does that."

"And what did you attribute it to before I came along?"

"Well, a man has needs. What can I say?"

"And how did you satisfy those needs before I came along?"

"I usually spent a bit of quality time by myself."

"Was it as satisfying that way?"

"Maybe not as satisfying, but it let me find out how good I am at this." *That grin.*

"That's not fair. I don't have anyone else to compare you to."

"Oh, Lacy, hon, there's no comparison. Now come over here and see to your man."

She thought he was probably right. No other man could possibly compare to Emmett, and he belonged to her. She took one step back then pushed off with the other foot and went flying through the air, landing on top of him. Emmett yelled out in surprise and the force bounced the headboard against the wall. They both started laughing.

"I wonder what your mother thought when she heard that."

"Probably that we're being playful."

"So much for trying to be quiet," he said.

"We can try to be quiet, starting now."

"I don't know. Maybe we should convince her that your husband is wild about you. That he can't keep away from you. That he loves to hear all those moans and pleas and screams that come out of your mouth. Yes, ma'am, that's it. I'm going to make you scream."

"Emmett, no, please, you know I can't help it. It'll be embarrassing. Please?" She drew out the word pleadingly.

He pulled her face down and kissed the tip of her nose. "You know I have a hard time saying no to you, girl. All right, I won't make it my mission to make you scream. I'll just, you know, do some things to you and if you just happen to scream, you can't blame me." He held his hands out as if to show innocence. He grinned. "But I don't promise I won't pump you so hard, the bed bangs against the wall and she thinks there's an earthquake."

In a quick motion, he grabbed her and turned them over, so he was on top. "Reach up and grab the spindles."

"What?"

"I don't want your hands getting in the way. So grab a headboard spindle with each one and hold on."

"Oh." She reached up and found a spindle with each hand. *This is new.*

"Now, I have you captive and you can't get loose. You can't move while I kiss right here." He bent down to kiss that sweet spot at the base of her neck. The kiss turned into a sucking sensation and she whined at the intensity. "I love what this does to you."

His hands slowly made their way down to her breasts and his mouth followed. The low moan he made as he sucked one nipple seemed to add vibration. He went to the other one while his hand took over on the one his mouth just left. He tickled all around, gently squeezed in undulating movements, then concentrated on her nipples. He gently rolled them slightly between his thumbs and forefingers. He twisted them just a little bit, only enough to give a hint of the pain she'd feel if he continued. He pinched them. First lightly, then harder, then a little harder. She began to make whimpering sounds. He flicked them with the tip of his finger, then with a finger-nail. Her whimpering had some little gasps and cries mixed in.

"I love the sounds you make. Seeing you like this makes me hard as a rock. You go on and make all those little noises you want to. She won't hear these."

Emmett continued tormenting her nipples and her mewling got a little louder. That made him want to torment her even more.

He reached down between her legs and let out a low, sexy chuckle. "Damn, girl, you're wet as a river down here."

Her breath was already labored. "I can't help it."

"I know you can't. Told you I was good, didn't I?"

Lacy grinned but still registered protest. "Please, I'm ready for you. I need you inside me."

"In just a little bit. I want to play a little more."

Emmett kissed a nipple and sucked up as much of her breast as would fit in his mouth. Then he sucked. Hard.

Lacy's head began to turn left and right on her pillow. Perspiration began to bead up on her skin.

He ran his fingers between her legs to wet them, then he started teasing her little bud, already swollen and sensitive. Her moans became breathy little words like *oh* and *yes*, and they got louder as he continued. Emmett felt a hand stroking his hair and he stopped.

"I told you to hold on to the spindles, darlin'."

"I forgot. It feels so good."

"I'm glad it feels good, but hold on to the spindles."

"All right." She grabbed them again.

He lowered himself and put his mouth at her bud. He licked it with the flat of his tongue, letting the rough texture tease her. His mouth rounded and he sucked, teasing the little pearl with the tip of his tongue.

Lacy rotated her hips almost in a figure eight, and Emmett quickened the pace of his tongue. He was enjoying the sounds of her excitement until he felt her hand on him again.

"Lacy, hold on to the spindles."

She made a sound of frustration. "Are you punishing me?"

Emmett stopped completely and sat up. He shook his head as if shaking something off his face and ran his fingers through his hair. "If you have to ask that, darlin', then I'm doing something wrong."

"You aren't; it feels wonderful, so wonderful it's almost too much for me to take. I want you inside me. I want to hold you inside me."

"You will, baby, you will. I want that, too. But first, I want to play. I want you at my mercy. That's how I want you to feel—powerless. If I wanted to punish you, I'd go get that wooden spoon. Now can you hold on to the spindles for me?"

"I'll try."

Emmett got up off the bed. "Try's not good enough." He went to her dresser drawer and pulled out a couple of her stockings. When he came back to her, he tied each wrist to a spindle as far apart as she could reach.

"There. Now you're at my mercy. All right, where was I?"

She waggled her bottom, inviting his attention, but he really didn't need her guidance. Emmett returned his mouth to her pearl and put two fingers inside her. Soon she was not only making the same noises she had been, but they were louder, and she was struggling against her bonds.

"You'd better watch the noise level, darlin'," he said, both amused and smugly satisfied.

She whimpered, as loud as whimpers go.

The tempo of his fingers thrusting inside her quickened and her body bucked up to meet each one. Emmett sucked on her little nub and he recognized the signals that told him she was nearly there. He stopped.

Lacy groaned and pulled at her wrists. "Emmett, please, I need you."

"I know, baby. Just a little more. Just think how good it'll be when I finally let you spend."

Her voice was pitiful. "Please, do it now."

His hands went back to her nipples, rubbing and then flicking them. He'd noticed how that made her hot. She tried to shake him off and pulled hard at the wrist ties. She was sweating.

Emmett chuckled. "Damn good thing I made this headboard myself. If anyone else had made it, I'd be afraid it might come apart."

Her eyes widened. "Emmett, did you make the headboard with this in mind?"

He gave her a devilish smirk. "And the footboard, too. We can try that another time."

"I can't take any more, Emmett, please! I'm begging you."

"I like it when you beg, darlin'."

Emmett grabbed a pillow and lifted her enough to slide it under her bottom to give him a better angle. The desperate need in her eyes took him to his edge, too. It was a powerful link between them. He positioned himself on his knees between her legs, his length in his right hand while his left teased her little pearl again. She was so needy, she used the little leverage she gained through her hold on the spindles to try to push herself toward him.

She was sweating. She was panting. She could think of nothing but getting him inside her. "Please. Now. Please."

Emmett moved a little and placed the mushroom head, almost touching her. He looked up at her and grinned perversely.

Lacy struggled at the ties again. "Please. Now." It was a plaintive cry.

"Please what, darlin'?" He eased the very tip in then pulled it back out. Then he did it again.

"Tell me what you want."

Lacy let out an anguished cry. "Fuck me," she screamed.

Emmett did exactly that. Hard, fast, forceful, almost violent, his thrusts were enough to make the bed repeatedly hit the wall. Both their cries and shouts built and rang out until Lacy's body arched in a fierce climax and Emmett allowed himself to follow her. He collapsed on top of her and rolled over so she wouldn't have to bear his weight, especially since she could barely catch her breath.

In a minute or so, he freed her hands then got up to bring them cool, wet cloths. He brought them a glass of water, too.

When they had cooled off and calmed down, Emmett

turned to her. "How are we going to face your mother in the morning?"

Lacy chuckled then sighed in resignation. "She'll probably applaud."

"Do you realize you finally said *fuck*?" She heard the humor in his voice. "Kind of loud."

She groaned and closed her eyes, thinking of her mother hearing that word from her. "Oh, fuck."

———

THE NEXT MORNING, the young couple was awakened early by sounds coming from the kitchen. Emmett put on the clothes he picked up from the floor that he'd worn the day before and Lacy put on her robe.

She stood facing the closed door, her hand on the knob. "I guess we have to face her sometime. Might as well get it over with."

When she opened the door, the smell of coffee and bacon met them. In the kitchen, the table was already set for breakfast. Butter and jelly were on the table, as were glasses and a pitcher of milk. Three cups sat on the table with cream and sugar nearby. Amelia was whisking a bowl of eggs.

"Oh, I didn't mean to wake you up, but it is good timing. I just put biscuits in the oven."

"Mother, you didn't have to do all this."

"No, but I wanted to. No one has let me do any work since I've been out here. I know it's early, but I didn't want to be late for church. I wasn't paying close attention to the time when you brought me out here," she said apologetically.

"It's not too early for us," Emmett said. "Besides, I'll get up in the wee hours if you're going to cook like this."

"Emmett, I'll cook for you," Lacy said almost defensively. "I just, you know, haven't really had occasion to yet."

He grinned and kissed her on the cheek, then he poured coffee into the three cups on the table.

"Mother, what can I do to help?"

"Nothing, I don't think. This is a well-organized kitchen. I found everything I needed."

"I'll do all the cleanup," Lacy said.

"We should leave here at about ten. That'll get us there in plenty of time to visit before the sermon starts."

"Oh, good," Amelia said. "I never liked to rush when getting ready to go somewhere."

"Mother, if we have time, will you fix my hair in that braided style with a bun the way Sylvie's mother used to fix hers? I've never been able to do that and make mine look decent."

"Of course, I will," Amelia said, smiling. "It'll be like old times again."

"Show me how to do it," Emmett said. "Then I can fix it for her."

They both looked at him with a new perspective.

"Lacy, you married yourself a wonderful man."

"I'm learning that. More and more by the minute, it seems."

After breakfast, Amelia stood and excused herself. As she walked toward her room, she said, "I want to take a quick bath." She stopped and turned back to face them with a big smile on her face. "I don't think I've ever said the words 'quick bath' before. I tell you what, hot running water on tap makes all the difference."

AT CHURCH, Emmett introduced Lacy and Amelia to several people before Charlotte stole Amelia away. Gann came up and joined the couple. He gave Lacy a big hug and told her again how happy he was to have her in the family.

They went on inside and found a pew in the middle where there was room for all three of them.

"Is it always this crowded?" Lacy asked.

"It's getting that way," Gann answered. He lowered his voice. "Right now, this building is both the church and school-house. So far, the subject hasn't come up in our deacon's meet-ings, but the way this town's growing, we need to expand. I've been thinking about paying for a new church building if the men are willing to contribute labor. Then we can convert this building into a dedicated schoolhouse."

"That's a wonderful idea, Gann. And generous of you," Lacy whispered.

"It's important to the town's growth."

"Let me split the cost with you," Emmett said. "And of course, I'll provide any metalwork that's needed."

Gann grinned. "I already planned for you to do both of those things. Maybe you'll get yourself here with a little more regularity."

AFTER THE SERVICE, Emmett invited the Copperfields and the Smitherses and his uncle to join them at Mary's restau-rant. They agreed to, of course, and for Amelia and the Copperfields, it would be one last chance to visit before Amelia had to leave to go home.

Emmett, Lacy, and Amelia arrived first, just in time to see a clearly resolute man exit the building. He held a woman by her upper arm, half dragging and half propelling her forward.

"You have it coming, Martha. You were warned."

"Please, Jack, not that. At least lower your voice."

"If you didn't want people to know, perhaps you shouldn't have acted so rudely in public."

"I promise I won't act like that again. I promise."

"You've made that promise before, and I made the mistake of believing you."

Emmett pursed his lips to keep from smirking just in case the couple looked up at them. So far, they didn't seem to notice that they weren't alone as they walked toward the hotel. There were several rigs outside the restaurant, so at least his wagon wasn't directly in or beside their path.

"Can we wait until we get back home? It's only a few days. Please, Jack. I promise I won't argue or fight you when it's time."

"No. I prefer to handle it now. You're lucky I didn't do it in the restaurant."

"But the hotel, Jack. People will hear."

"I imagine they will."

They were out of earshot by then, but the three watched them until they entered the hotel.

"What, um, what's going to happen to that woman?"

Emmett was about to answer her, but Amelia did. "I do believe a misbehaving wife is about to get her backside blistered."

"Oh, surely not," Lacy said slowly, not wanting to believe it.

"You heard them with your own ears, dear," Amelia said. Then she added, "I can recall having similar conversations with George when we first married."

Lacy gasped and whipped her head around to look at her mother. "You, Mother? Father... did that to you?"

Amelia laughed. "I had a very smart mouth on me when I was young."

"But you let him hit you?"

"Hit me? A well-deserved thrashing isn't the same as 'hitting me,'" she said. "Your father would never have hurt me, not by any stretch. Punishment and correction aren't abuse, dear. And, Emmett," she said as she looked at him, "you have our blessing to take care of Lacy in this manner if the situation arises."

"I appreciate that," he answered.

Nothing else was said because the others arrived. Lacy was quiet as they walked in and sat down.

As with most conversations that Harriet Smithers took part in, the conversation turned to Operation Big Rock Brides, the mail order bride efforts undertaken by the Ladies' Aid Society.

"Gann Douglas," she pointed at him good-naturedly, "I've been waiting for you to come to me asking for a bride. Now that you've seen what a good job we can do, I imagine you'll be interested in getting a bride for yourself."

He laughed. "Now Harriet, I've always thought I'd find a wife the old-fashioned way."

"How," she joked, "by clubbing her on the head and dragging her by her hair back to your cave while she's unconscious?"

"Well, it apparently worked for our ancestors."

"Apparently, there were available women back then," she said. "Look around this town. I don't see any available women."

"You do have a point there," he conceded. "How about if I think about it?"

"Just let me know when you're ready."

WHEN LUNCH WAS OVER, Charlotte hugged Amelia again and promised to be at the stage line the next day to see her off.

As Emmett drove the wagon down the street, Lacy asked

him to show her and her mother his blacksmith shop before they headed home.

"All right," he said as he pulled the team to a stop.

He helped the ladies down and pulled his key ring out of his pocket as he neared the front door. They'd both been in blacksmith shops before, but none looked like this. It had the fire and metal smell of other shops, but the similarities ended there. It was a large space that had been divided into different areas. They weren't exactly different rooms because the walls didn't go all the way across. There were walls that connected to the sides of the space, but they didn't meet in the middle. There was a wide open space that allowed a spacious entry into the work area; it gave the feeling of both separation and openness.

The front room was big and looked like a showroom for finished products. It had a counter that was clearly for dealing with customers, but at the far end, it had some rasps and knives and items they recognized as farrier supplies. Around the walls hung completed works. Mostly, there were horseshoes of various sizes and widths. There were belt buckles. There were several specialty hardware items that weren't carried in the mercantile, such as ornamental hinges and door plates and items required for plumbing. There were nails, bolts and washers, and other fasteners. There were a couple of weathervanes. There were some other items the ladies didn't recognize, but they assumed they were parts for machines of some sort. There was a plow and a sickle by one wall. There were axe heads, hammer heads, and some metal picks. There were also axes and hammers that were already attached to wooden handles. There were other tools that Emmett explained had been requested by the copper mine workers. Wheel rims and long iron plates were on one long shelf. There were candle holders, both plain and fanciful, and fireplace tools and fittings.

The women were amazed.

"Emmett, you made all these things?" Lacy asked.

"I did indeed."

"What do you make the most?"

"That's easy; it's horseshoes. I keep a good stock because of the stagecoach. When they need one, they're always in a hurry."

"What if you aren't here when they need you?" Lacy thought of all the days he'd stayed home, and of what would happen if a horseshoe was needed while they were on their honeymoon.

"Bill Taggert at the stagecoach office has a key. So does Gann, by the way. I showed Bill how to light the forge so he can adjust the shoes if he needs to. Most of the time, though, shoes fit the horse right off the rack if they use a rasp or something to reshape the horse's hoof."

He showed them the middle room that held the sort of equipment and tools they were accustomed to seeing at a blacksmith's shop. Lacy looked over at the wall and noticed two doors that met so that when they were opened, it would be a very large opening. "I don't remember seeing doors on the outside of the building."

"That's because I didn't want a way for them to be opened from the outside. It gets mighty hot in here with that forge going, and I have to have ventilation for me and to keep the fire going. So I open the doors and that window to get a crosswind." He pointed at a window on the opposite wall.

"What's in that back room?"

"That's where I can do more detailed pieces, and I have more equipment for working with metals other than iron." He grinned. "I made our rings back there."

"Where does that door go?" Amelia asked, pointing to a door in the back corner.

He grinned again. "To the outhouse."

SEVEN

The week passed quickly. After Amelia boarded the stagecoach on Monday, Lacy concentrated on packing for their long honeymoon trip. She fretted over what to take and what not to take, and Emmett reminded her he planned to buy her many things on the trip, so it didn't matter if she forgot items.

"I fully expect to have to buy new trunks and have them shipped home."

He finally convinced her to pack a reasonable selection of her favorite clothes, and his, which meant she packed all her skimpy nighties. Lacy decided on her own not to pack her bags completely full, so she'd have room for purchases. Maybe they wouldn't have to buy new bags that way. Emmett laughed at her. "We can afford new bags."

Friday arrived. Gann came by in the wagon to take them to town, to save them the trouble of leaving their horses and wagon at the livery. He reminded them several times to wire him about when they'd return home so he could meet them. After they unloaded the baggage, he gave Lacy a big hug and Emmett a handshake that turned into a hug.

"You two have the best honeymoon ever, and please give

Amelia and your father my best. Don't worry about anything here; I'll take care of everything."

"Thank you, Gann," Lacy said. "Oh, don't forget to stop and take all our perishable food home. I tried to use up all I could, but there are still some things left."

"I'll go do that on my way back. You two have a good trip now."

Emmett checked in at the desk in the stage office and then went back outside to wait with Lacy on one of the benches provided. They were soon joined by another couple Emmett knew who were also traveling to Laramie.

"Lacy, this is Deacon Snow and his wife Tillie. Deacon and his brother Reed are private detectives and actually, so is Tillie, I believe. Deacon, Tillie, this is my wife, Lacy."

They went through the normal introductory pleasantries and discovered in the conversation that Deacon and Tillie had wrapped up a case for a client in Laramie, and the man wanted the final report in person. There was a possibility of another case for the man. The Snows decided to make the trip a little getaway vacation and would be staying in Laramie for a few days.

"Emmett! Lacy!" a female voice called out from a passing buggy. She kept hollering while her husband pulled to a stop. It was Harriet and Arthur Smithers.

"I'm so glad we caught you before the stage got here. We were just on our way out to your house with a little wedding gift."

Emmett stood and rushed over to help Harriet down off the buggy. She was perfectly capable of getting down by herself, but she loved the attention. She loved attention from Emmett even more. It didn't matter that they were both happily married. Emmett just had that effect on women and Harriet wasn't immune.

Arthur stepped down and picked up a wooden box from the back seat, and he, Harriet and Emmett walked over to the covered walkway where Lacy was sitting. Harriet and Arthur greeted the Snows and Harriet sat down beside Lacy.

"Lacy and Emmett," she said, looking up at him, "we have a little gift we think every newlywed couple needs. Arthur and I have been giving one of these to all our mail order couples."

They were looking at Lacy and everyone missed the knowing grins on the faces of the Snows.

Arthur handed the box to Lacy. "Oh, another gift isn't necessary, Harriet. You've already done so much for us."

Lacy started to open the box, but Harriet put her hand on it to stop her. "You should open this sometime when you're alone together. Maybe in your hotel, or even in your Pullman on the train. Arthur and I usually like to visit with the couple when they open it and share our story and our philosophy and what we believe to be the secret of our marital success. Since you're leaving now, perhaps we can visit when you return."

"We would love to have you visit us. I look forward to it," Lacy said. "And thank you so much for the gift. I'm sure we'll love it."

The Snows struggled to keep straight faces.

"I certainly do hope you will," Harriet said as she stood up. "We'll talk about it later when you're settled back in after your trip. Arthur, I think we should leave now. It's just about time for the stage, and we don't want to be in the way."

"Harriet's right. We wish you all safe and happy travels," Arthur said, smiling as he took Harriet's arm and led her back to the wagon.

"I'll take that, darlin'," Emmett said. "There's room for it in my bag."

THE STAGE WASN'T AS PACKED as it usually was. In addition to the Burkes and the Snows, there were an older couple and a single salesman who were through-passengers. When the stage got underway, they all introduced themselves. The older couple, the Templetons, were only traveling as far as Rawlins so they wouldn't be on the eastbound train with the rest of them.

The salesman, Fred Willinger, was going on to Cheyenne. When he told them he'd never been there before except for an overnight stop once, Emmett said he'd grown up in Cheyenne and knew it well. He told the man all about the best restaurants, the best hotel to stay in, and what he thought was the best saloon.

The Snows said they hadn't spent much time in Laramie before, and they asked Lacy for her opinion on the same types of things, except for the saloon. Tillie wanted to know specifically about clothes shopping and Lacy recommended Handel's Dress Shop, her favorite. She told them she'd bought several new things before her move to Big Rock, and she'd bought them all at Handel's.

Emmett laughed. "If that's the case, then I can heartily recommend Handel's, too."

Lacy was a little embarrassed.

"Do you know how long you'll be in Laramie?" Deacon asked.

"We really don't," Emmett said. "I'd like to stay long enough to spend some time with Lacy's parents and get to know them. Our tentative plan is to go on to Cheyenne, but we'd both be fine to stay in Laramie the whole time, too."

"Will you be staying at a hotel or with Lacy's family?"

Lacy answered that. "I want to stay with my family, at least for a couple of days, to visit with Father." She looked at

Emmett. "We hadn't talked about where we'd stay. Is that all right with you?"

"It's fine with me. I don't want to be an unwelcome guest, though. Let's do plenty of cooking and cleanup for your mother."

"Well," Deacon said, "if you have spare time and want to go out to eat or to the theater or anything like that, we're staying at the Belmont Hotel." He added, "Or if you ladies would like to go shopping while Emmett and I have a cigar and drinks."

Lacy shared the address of her parents just in case they wanted to contact them.

THE OVERNIGHT STOP in Cooper's Gap didn't have enough accommodations for several couples, so they had a dormitory style room for men and another for the women. Emmett wasn't happy with the arrangement, but he didn't complain to anyone other than Lacy.

"Fair warning, girlie, when we get on that train in our private Pullman unit, we're going to make up for lost time. I don't like being separated for a whole night."

"All right, but you need to remember the beds on the train aren't as well-built as our iron one you made. You'll need to hold your enthusiasm somewhat in check."

He laughed. "The hell I will. I'm rich. I'll buy 'em a new bed."

That night when Lacy and Tillie were tucked in their cots, they chatted a bit.

"How long have you and Deacon been married?"

"Just a few months."

"Then you're still newlyweds, too. Were you one of their mail order brides?"

"No, Deacon and I met on a train to San Francisco. But my cousin, Nessa, was the first one."

"Nessa Kelly? She played the piano at our wedding ceremony. I like her. I told Emmett we should have her and her husband out for dinner sometime. Or meet them in town. I'd like to get to know more people."

"Oh, I know they'd like that. When we get back, let's see if we can arrange something. We can all get together for an evening. You know it's funny, when we were small, we lived in Omaha and Nessa and I were really close. Then her family moved to Baltimore and her best friend there was named Bethie. Here's the amazing part—Bethie also lives in Big Rock now. Her husband has a big ranch outside of town."

"What a coincidence! I suppose it really is a small world in some ways. Now who is Nessa's husband?"

"Angus Kelly. He's a great big bear of a man, I think he's about six foot eight. Red hair. But he's one of the nicest people I've ever met. His Irish accent's fun to listen to. He's a part owner of the sawmill and furniture store. As a matter of fact, he made... oh never mind, it isn't important."

"No, what were you going to say?"

Tillie waved her hand in dismissal. "Really, it isn't worth talking about. Just forget I said anything."

Lacy turned on her side to look at Tillie with a mischievous grin. "No, no, you can't do that. Tell me what you were going to say. Angus made what?"

Tillie sighed in good-humored resignation. "All right, he made the gift you got today from Harriet and Arthur. But you can't let on that I told you about it."

"What is it?" Lacy asked.

"No, ma'am, I won't spoil a gift surprise."

"Then tell me how you know what it is."

"Because Angus made one for us, too. And that's all I'll say."

"Really? You won't tell me what it is?"

"No, I won't. But if you want to talk about it after you open it, I will. In private, though."

Lacy couldn't imagine what the gift could possibly be.

———

AT RAWLINS, they all bid goodbye to the Templetons. There was just enough time to get a quick dinner before boarding the train. There was no dining car, but there was a car where light refreshments, coffee, and water were available.

On this train, the configuration was different than the one Lacy rode to Big Rock. This one had only two sleeping units per Pullman car rather than the three as had the other train. The units were larger and more comfortable with the extra room to spread out.

The porter came in to prepare their bed and let them know when the train would stop for the next day's morning meal. Other stops along the way would be simply for water and coal and possibly additional passengers. The man said goodnight and he hoped they could sleep through them.

Emmett grabbed Lacy and surprised her, pulling her into his arms. "I hope you're ready, darlin', I saved up all my energy for an earthshattering fuck."

"You and that word!" she said.

"I remember making you say it."

"Yes," she smiled and ran her fingers over his lips, "you certainly did."

Lacy pulled his jacket off and hung it from a hook. Next, she pushed him down on the padded bench and knelt to take off his shoes and socks. They were set aside. She stood and unbuttoned his shirt while she looked at him with a flirtatious grin, and he grinned back at her with growing anticipation. She hung the shirt on the same hook with the jacket. She stroked his chest and teased his nipples with her tongue while she unfastened his britches. They were folded and set on the far end of the bench.

"My turn now," Emmett said while reaching for her buttons.

"Nah ah ah," she said. "I'm not through having my turn yet."

She knelt again and pushed his thighs apart enough to give her access to him. She took his length in her hand and brought her face down to the tip. When her tongue made contact, she heard the gravelly moan and reached for his sac. Her lips teased it and she gently sucked each soft stone into her mouth and tongued it until Emmett's leg bounced and he could only mutter, "Oh, darlin'." When he put his hand on her head, she backed up.

"Not this time, baby," she said. "I want you to hold your hands out of the way. Can you do that for me?"

"Oh, ho ho." It came out of his mouth in a low voice as if to say, 'Surely, you aren't trying to get even with me."

"I wondered what it would be like to have control of this little episode. I can only count on your honor since I can't tie you to a headboard here. If you have trouble keeping your hands away, maybe you could lace your fingers behind your head." It was an innocent look that she gave him.

"I'll accept this challenge. And you should know, little girl, that when I succeed, I shall exact retribution for this."

"You'll have to succeed first."

Lacy lowered her mouth back to his length while her left hand cupped his sac again and rolled it just a little. Emmett's hands were on the bench. She flicked her tongue all around the mushroom head then circled it. She put her lips on it and sucked while her tongue continued to tease, and she did it down the length of him, to his groin and back up again. She raised herself a little higher so she could take more of him in her mouth with wet sucks as she went.

Emmett was holding his breath and she saw his hands curled into fists. Lacy felt powerful. With him in her mouth, she freed her hands to explore and tickle his inner thighs, his hair, and the tender area between his sac and his brown pucker. She even rubbed a finger over it and pushed slightly as though she planned to insert it. He moaned again, long, strained moans, and his fists pounded the bench. She looked up and saw that his eyes were clenched shut as though he were in distress.

Lacy pulled back and approached the shaft again, with soppy, wet licks. Her fingers reached up and tweaked his nipples, gently at first, then not so gently. She pinched. She twisted just a little bit, then flicked again. His chest jerked in little spasms, but he didn't open his eyes. He did break out in a sweat, though.

She brought her hands back down, trailing them softly down his torso. Taking his sac again, she made the same motions as before, only a little faster, then put her hand around the shaft base as far as it would go and began a slight undulation as she moved it up and down without lifting her hand from his skin. Her mouth took his length in as far as it would fit, and she matched it to the movements of her hand. As she quickened her pace, Emmett made those sounds that she recognized as signaling his climax.

She stopped her efforts and sat back, loosening her grip on his member.

"Come on, darlin', that's it, I'm almost there. Feels so good," he coaxed in that sexy whisper of his.

She whispered back, "But think how much more powerful it'll feel if you wait just a little longer."

His eyes flew open and looked at her with a flash of some

emotion she couldn't identify for sure. He smirked at her and slowly shook his head. "You will pay."

"Just keep your hands out of my way."

She still held his sac and squeezed it just a bit. He moaned. Or was it a groan? Lacy turned her attention back to his hardness, but she started with playful tongue jabs that felt good but didn't propel him toward orgasm. She made her way down to the base and began to lick and flick the skin of his groin that her fingers had explored before then parted his legs more so she could reach under his sac.

Emmett was no longer quiet. The sounds from him weren't coherent, but they were louder than his moans had been earlier. She flicked her tongue on that tender spot again, and he finally managed a coherent word, "Fuck." It was loud.

Lacy lifted her head and saw his arms in the air, fists tight, arms tense, and his corded veins threatening to burst. She whispered, "Just a little bit more for me, baby. Think how intense and extreme it's going to feel if you build up that need a little more."

This time, it was a growl that came from him and his tensed arms trembled in the air.

She felt him push his feet into the floor and his back against the seat. Lacy knew he couldn't last much longer. She'd never seen him last this long.

She flicked around the head a little more, teasing little flicks that had him gasping within the growls. She felt the telltale tightening of his sac and plunged her head down on him, her tongue dancing around his sensitive skin. Her head bounced up and down, and she sucked harder each time on the outstroke. The pitch of the sounds he made rose and intensified, and she gently squeezed his sac again.

It was a long drawn out sound he made, not really a word and not really a moan. Lacy continued to suck as he spent in her mouth, swallowing more than once to catch it all. She continued the tender licks, cleaning him with her tongue, and then she knelt back up, smiling.

Emmett panted and wiped the sweat from his forehead. He opened his eyes and started to speak but couldn't just yet. He held up his finger, an indication for her to wait for him to recover enough to talk. Her smile turned into a smirk.

"As soon as I can move again, your ass is mine, darlin'."

Lacy put on the innocent façade again and sat there, making a show of patiently waiting. She held out her hands and checked her fingernails. She tucked a few stray hairs behind her ear. She demurely smoothed out some wrinkles in her skirt.

Suddenly, she felt herself rise and realized he had the collar and upper part of her shirtwaist in his fist and was pulling her up by it. He let go of her top and patted it as if he was sorry for doing it. He wasn't sorry. He reached up and ripped apart her blouse and buttons flew everywhere. He found the button on her waistband and yanked it off, pushing the skirt down. Her petticoat was next, and he pulled the ribbon hard, but it didn't rip. He pushed it down her legs. Lacy backed away, not totally sure he was doing this in fun. Her shift had a button placket on the top five or six inches and he ripped off the buttons, grabbed each side, yanked, and the shift ripped all the way down. She backed away again as he reached for her bloomers. She couldn't escape him, though, and soon they were at her feet, too. She stepped out of them and away but there was nowhere to run in the little compartment.

"I've got you, little girl, you can't get away from me."

He was upon her in two steps, but she bent down and darted beside and behind him.

"You're just making it worse for yourself," he said in a sing-song voice and she knew then he was doing it in fun.

"You have to catch me first," she sing-songed right back at him.

"The harder you make me work, the harder it'll be."

"You mean your mighty oak?"

"I mean the spanking you just earned for yourself."

"Didn't that feel good for you?"

"It felt good beyond my wildest dreams."

"Then why are you spanking me? You should reward me."

The two of them stood about, each balancing on alternating feet, ready for the other to make a move. He chased her in the small space.

"Maybe I'll spank you for not having done that sooner. Or maybe, just maybe, the spanking could be your reward."

"I don't think it works that way." She darted behind him again, escaping his grasp.

The train braked slightly then lurched forward and she lost her balance. She fell over with her head and chest on the bed, legs sprawled out behind her in a less than dignified way. Emmett saw his chance and took it. Before she could get up, he had his hand on her back, holding her down.

"It would seem that divine providence thinks you need a spankin'. You are in a prime position for it, darlin'. For other things, too, but right now that ass looks ripe for a good lickin' and I plan to deliver a fine one." His hands roamed all over her back and cheeks and thighs.

"No, please, Emmett. Not that."

"Yes, that." He stepped to her left and kept his left arm holding her down. He started little love pats on her cheeks.

"Wait! We should open that gift from Harriet and Arthur. They said to open it when we were alone."

"We can open it anytime. You're just trying to stall."

"No, I really want to open the gift and see what it is."

"You aren't going to get out of this."

"She wanted us to open it."

"All right. We can open it. Then we get back to the business," he paused, "at my hand."

She let out a little groan and rose so she could sit down. Emmett opened his suitcase and pulled out the box. He handed it to her and sat down on the bed beside her.

"It's a pretty box," she said.

He agreed.

She opened it and found something wrapped in pretty paper. Emmett took the box and set it out of the way while she unwrapped it. When it finally was free of the paper, she looked at Emmett in surprise and dismay. It was a wooden paddle with *Obey* carved into one side of it and *Lacy* carved into the other side, both in reversed script.

Emmett burst out laughing and took it from her. "You see, darlin'? It was ordained. Fate. An inescapable, inevitable, predestined event. Now. Up. I think I want you over my knees for this."

EIGHT

Laramie, Wyoming Territory

Emmett hired transport in Laramie instead of renting a rig just yet. Lacy said they could most likely use her father's. He agreed, thinking he could always hire a buggy later if they decided they wanted one or if they decided to move to a hotel.

When they pulled up at Lacy's former home, the driver helped Emmett unload the bags. Emmett paid him, including a generous tip, and the man's face lit up. He wished them a wonderful day.

Lacy had a happy look on her face as she took his hand, took a deep breath, and opened the door. The sight that greeted them frightened her speechless.

Amelia looked bedraggled, struggling under the weight of her pale and drawn husband, his arm around her shoulder for support. Emmett ran to the man's other side and put his arm around him and under his opposite arm, taking the weight off Amelia and taking most of it off George's own feet.

"Help me get him back in bed; it's this way."

Once they had him in the bed again, it took George a few

minutes to regain his breath. "You must be Emmett," he finally said.

Emmett sat down beside him and smiled. "Yes, sir, I am. I'm pleased to finally meet you."

"Likewise, young man. I was awfully uneasy about this quick marriage, even though I knew it would help her situation here. When Amelia told me about you, I felt like a prayer had been answered. She thinks highly of you."

"I'll do my best to live up to it, sir. I think highly of her, too."

"Please, call me George. Lacy? Come over here. Let me see you while I still can."

Amelia addressed the puzzled look on Lacy's face. "The past two days, his vision has gotten bad. He says it's sometimes too blurry to tell what's what."

Lacy took his hand and Emmett pulled her down to sit on his lap. "I'm here, Father."

"Princess, you and your mother have been my sunshine all these years. I remember when you were a little thing, running to me when I came in the house. The love in your eyes would make me cry sometimes and I'd have to turn my face away so you wouldn't see. I don't think I ever told you that. I wondered what I had done in my life that was good enough to deserve you both. You made me want to do my best."

The tears came to Lacy's eyes.

"Doc Jones thinks this is the same sickness I had a couple of years ago, but this time it's come back so bad, it's going to take me. Now, now, no, don't cry. I don't want you to be sad. You need to be happy for all the good times we had. That's how I want you to remember me, you hear? Not like this, like a sick, feeble man in bed. Remember when I used to throw you up in the air and you'd squeal?"

The tears were falling down her face unchecked. "I remember. I'd beg you to do it, again and again."

"You sure did. And I did it, until I thought my arms would fall off, but I didn't want to stop and disappoint you."

Lacy's heart was breaking. "You never disappointed me, Father."

"I love you, princess. Never forget that."

"I love you, too. You don't forget that, either."

"I won't. Bible says there's no sadness in Heaven, so I expect I'll only remember the good things. You and Amelia are the very best things that ever happened to me."

George tried to focus on Emmett's face. "Emmett, I have to ask something of you. Man to man."

"What is it, sir?"

"I want you to promise me you'll take care of my girls. Both of them."

Emmett fought tears, too. "It would be my honor, sir. I promise you I'll take care of them. Neither of them will ever want for anything."

"Amelia's going to need a lot of help in these next few weeks. All kinds of help."

"I'll be here for her. For them both."

"Thank you, son." He paused. "You two be sure to tell my grandchildren about me. Tell them I love them from Heaven."

"We will, Father."

"Good." He took Amelia's hand in his weak one. "When the time comes, you let me go. I'm ready. I don't want you to waste time mourning me. I'd rather you be happy for the time we had. I'm happy for it. I treasure the love we had. I know you'll be sad for a little while, I guess that's natural, but don't wallow in it. Promise me, no widow's weeds. I want you to get on with your life. Start over. You're a beautiful, vibrant woman. The best thing you can do to honor the love we had is to live the life every woman should have. You are my best friend." He squeezed her hand as much as he could. "You'll find a new best friend."

George was worn out from the exertion of speaking so much and it wasn't long before he lapsed into sleep.

In the kitchen, Lacy put on a pot of water for tea. She got out the cups and the sugar and cream and joined her mother and Emmett at the table.

"I'm sorry about the way you found out, that you were surprised like that," Amelia said, rubbing her eyes. "When I got home on Thursday, he was tired. He said he'd been tired for a couple of days. We didn't think much about it and chalked it up to him being lonely while I was gone. On Friday, he felt so bad, we didn't open the store, and he got worse as the day wore on. I sent the neighbor for Dr. Jones." She looked at the clock. "He'll be here directly. He's been coming by every day."

Lacy got up and got another cup for the doctor.

"George hasn't eaten anything since Friday night and I can barely get him to drink any water. He won't drink broth. His vision started failing yesterday. Or maybe the night before, it's all running together. Dr. Jones doesn't know any more about the disease than they knew two years ago. But we're certain he won't make it this time."

"I wish you could have gotten word to us, but I guess there was no time. We left the day you realized he was so bad," Lacy said.

"I knew you were coming today. George knew it, too. I believe he willed himself to live long enough to see you two."

In the quiet that followed, Lacy got up and poured the hot water into the teapot and brought it to the table to let it steep.

"Has he been in much pain?" Emmett asked.

"Some. He wouldn't take any laudanum, though. Said he didn't want to sleep away the time he had left."

Lacy teared up again. Emmett took both their hands and held them.

"I wish I could have known him better," Emmett said.

"He would have liked you," Amelia said, and she managed a smile.

"He called me son. No one's called me that since my pa died years ago. It sounded nice."

There was a light knock at the door and Amelia went to let the doctor in. Lacy started to pour tea, but thought it would be cold if they went to see her dad first. She and Emmett stood and waited for them to come in.

"Lacy, I'm so glad you made it here." He turned to Emmett and stuck out his hand. "I'm Doc Jones."

"Emmett Burke, sir. Pleased to meet you. I'm Lacy's husband."

"Yes, I know. I sure was proud to hear our girl got married to a good man. She's a fine young lady, you know."

"I do know that, sir." Emmett smiled at the doctor.

"I'm going to go peek in on George. Amelia said he drifted off to sleep again." He pointed to the table. "I wouldn't mind a cup of tea if that fourth cup's for me."

Lacy smiled at him. "It's ready. I'll pour it up as soon as you two come back in here."

They weren't gone very long. When she heard their foot-steps in the hall, she poured the tea and placed a cup at each chair. She'd forgotten stirring spoons and quickly got some to put on the table.

"What do you think, Dr. Jones?" Emmett asked once they all had a sip of tea.

"His pulse is thready and weak, and his lungs are struggling something pitiful. His heart's just played out and ready to quit. That last bout with this mess two years ago damaged his heart. Did him damage all over, but especially to his heart. You all need to be prepared. I don't expect him to live another day. He'll probably pass over in his sleep in the next few hours. As deaths go, that's the best way. He's not feeling any pain anymore."

Lacy couldn't stop the tears and Emmett handed her his handkerchief.

"I'll come back first thing in the morning. But before I leave, I need to tell you about something else. I'm sorry to make your sorrow and trouble even worse, but you need to know."

Lacy looked up at him, as did the others.

"When Mr. and Mrs. Nixon died, a nagging thought bothered me something fierce. I'd taken care of them through their illness until the very end. You know they were old. Both of them had an assortment of old people's complaints, and those didn't stop when they came down with this illness. They kept telling me the symptoms and I finally realized not all of them could be attributed to the new illness. Some were their old complaints or a worsening of them. When I helped the undertaker get them ready to take to the funeral parlor, I noticed a lot of hair on their pillows. A lot of hair. I went by the funeral home later to check my suspicion, and sure enough, if I ran my fingers through their hair, it came out in my hands. It was falling out by the handful. They both had bad feet anyway, but they kept telling me they were hurting and burning more than usual. I didn't figure it out until I saw all the hair coming out. I was careful to note down everything they said because I wanted to research something I'd heard about a long time ago. I'd never actually seen it."

"Never seen what, Dr. Jones?" Lacy asked.

"I wrote to a couple of other doctors I know, who had experience, and they confirmed what I thought. It couldn't be anything else. The Nixons died of arsenic poisoning. It was administered in small amounts so it would look like an illness that eventually led to death. Somebody murdered that old couple, and it was a cruel and miserable way to go."

"Have you told the authorities?" Emmett asked.

"I did, for all the good it did us. That pompous little deputy in charge of the investigation tried to lay it off on Lacy."

"Me? How could I have done it? I've never even been in their home."

"He said it would have only taken one time, but he's wrong. My word didn't faze him; he's sticking to his guns. He said you could have put arsenic in their sugar or something."

"That's absurd. Why didn't Carl get sick?"

"He said maybe Carl was your accomplice," the doctor answered.

"What is wrong with that man? He said I killed Carl with an accomplice. I don't understand why he's trying to accuse me of these things."

"Well, I might know something about that," Amelia said. "A year or so ago, he went to visit your father at the store. He puffed himself up, stated his case, and asked for George's blessing and permission to court you."

Lacy's face showed her revulsion. "That weaselly, sniveling, shriveled, pitiful excuse for a man."

"Your father had much the same reaction. He turned him down firmly."

"The deputy yelled at George and vowed we'd all be sorry, especially you. I'm afraid we dismissed it as sour grapes, but apparently you shouldn't underestimate a vengeful heart. We didn't want to tell you because the man is, well, so unseemly."

"Wait a minute. Are we talking about Deputy Faust? Elwin Faust?" Emmett asked.

"You know the deputy?"

"We are acquainted. We are not friends."

"I don't think he has any," the doctor said. "How did you meet him?"

"I lived here in Laramie for a few years before I moved to Big Rock. "Suffice it to say we had a run-in."

"Uh oh. Was this by any chance over a woman?" Lacy asked.

"It was, but not one I was interested in. He was interested in her. They were out at a restaurant, Rockwell's over on Fourth Street. I was alone at the next table and could hear them. He was telling her what she was and wasn't allowed to do in their relationship, or she would incur his wrath. She told him this was only their first date and if that was what he expected, there wouldn't be a second one. He slapped her, hard. It got the attention of everyone there and the young thing was terribly embarrassed. I got up and told him what I think about men who hit women. He clearly didn't like my opinion. That little runt stood up and threatened me. I stand six feet and four inches, and I towered over him. Most people would look at me and think I'm pretty strong and it might not be wise to pick a fight with me. Not Faust, though. He stuck out his chest and jutted out his chin and announced that I had insulted his honor and must pay for it."

"What happened?" Lacy was captivated by story.

"He pulled his gun and told me to pull mine."

"Did you?"

"Of course not. I grabbed his gun with my left hand and punched his jaw with my right. Knocked him flat out. The owner came out and thanked me for avoiding gunfire in his restaurant. I put the gun down on the table, paid for all our meals, and escorted the poor girl home." He shrugged. "Believe me, I know Deputy Faust."

"Well," the doctor said, "you might as well be ready to tangle with him. I'm sure he'll be here when he finds out Lacy's back in town."

"I can handle Faust."

"Maybe you can, but he's like a dog with a bone when he's got a point to make."

"How is Gerald Nixon?" Lacy asked.

"He's around, keeping a low profile."

"Do you know anything about Alan Huntsman? He was Carl's best friend."

The doctor got an odd look on his face. "Yes, he was, wasn't he? No, I don't believe I've seen him since Carl's funeral."

"Have they investigated any other people—other than Lacy?" Emmett asked.

"I gave the deputy my opinion of some I thought should be questioned. I think maybe he asked the cursory questions, like where they were on the day Carl died. To my knowledge, he didn't verify their stories. He's too focused on Lacy."

She shook her head. "That's pure lunacy."

"It is indeed. Listen, I'm going to go check on George again, then I'll be heading home. I'll be back in the morning. Send for me if you need me sooner."

Emmett nodded his head again.

When they were alone, Lacy turned to Emmett. "This is insane. When is he going to stop hassling me?"

"I can put a stop to that, but I do want to get to the bottom of this thing and figure out just who's who and what's what. The murders must be connected. I think we should go see Deacon and Tillie when we get a chance before they leave town. I'd like to hire them to investigate, since Faust isn't going to do it."

"Where's the sheriff in all this? Why does he put up with that man for a deputy?" Lacy asked.

"You mean Sheriff Faust?" Emmett asked.

"Oh, I get it now."

GEORGE DIED PEACEFULLY BEFORE DAWN. Amelia was at his side, dozing, but holding his hand. The sunrise woke her, and she knew immediately he was gone. When she touched him, he was still warm, and she knew he hadn't been gone long.

She let the newlyweds wake up on their own time; after all, there was nothing they could do. She covered his face with the sheet and went to cook breakfast.

Emmett and Lacy were up soon and came into the kitchen before stopping in George's room. The look on her mother's face told her. It wasn't a sad look; it was peaceful, serene and respectful. Lacy went into his room to say goodbye and kiss his cheek one last time and then she pulled the sheet back up.

"I know there's a lot to be done, and we want to do as much as we can for you. What can we do first?" Emmett asked Amelia.

"Doc Jones said he'd come by, so we don't need to notify him. We should let the pastor know. Once he knows, he'll spread the word and I imagine mourners will start coming to visit this afternoon. They always bring food."

"What about the store? Would you like for me to open it for a while and do some business?"

"No, I don't think so. But we should probably put a sign in the window about it being closed due to George's death. Emmett, in a few days, after the funeral, would you go with me to check the store? Get the cash and figure out where our accounts stand? George wasn't much for paperwork. Lacy can help with that, too."

"We'll be happy to do it. What else can we do?"

"I can't think right now. I can't even think of what needs to be done."

"All right, we'll figure it out as we go. The doc is coming this morning and he'll probably contact the funeral home. The pastor—we can go let the pastor know. We can do it right after breakfast. After that, I'd like to take Lacy and go see our friends who are staying at the Belmont. They're detectives from Big Rock and I trust them. They're in town wrapping up another case, and I want to hire them to get to the bottom of the Nixon murders. I can promise they'll do a much better job than the Fausts."

"That wouldn't take very much," Amelia offered.

"We can have all that taken care of and be back in the early afternoon. We'll notify the pastor, put a sign on the store, and go see the Snows. Will you be all right while we're gone?"

"Yes, I imagine the doctor will stay a while. He's been a good friend."

"I'm glad. I imagine George had a lot of friends, what with his business and the church. That should be comforting," Emmett offered.

"It is," Amelia said, smiling at Emmett and Lacy. "I feel so sorry for you two. This was supposed to be your honeymoon."

"Oh, Mother, that's not a problem at all. We can take a honeymoon anytime. I am just so glad we came in time to see Father before he passed away." Her eyes welled up again. "I feel guilty, because I had no idea his health was this bad. I would have tried to spend more time with him."

"He was glad you arrived in time to see him again, too, sweetheart. There's no need for you to feel any guilt, Lacy. He hadn't been this bad; it came upon him suddenly." Amelia looked around the room. "I just don't know what to do about everything. The store, the house, all of his things. I just don't know."

"You don't have to decide right now," Emmett said. "For the next few days, let's just do what we know needs to be done. Funerals can be stressful. We'll be here with you. You can decide what to do about the properties in your own time. There's no rush. I'll help you with all that. It's your decision, of course, but we'd like for you to come live with us."

"We do, Mother. It was Emmett's idea first."

Amelia finally let her tears fall.

"BEFORE WE HEAD to the Belmont, I want to stop at the telegraph office and send a wire to Gann and let him know what's happened."

"Good idea. I sure am glad he's there for us."

"Me, too, sweetie. Are you doing all right? This is something you can never be prepared for, and for it to come out of nowhere like this, you're probably reeling."

"I would never want him to linger in pain. He's better off. But it was awfully hard to tell him goodbye. We're lucky he didn't have a long, lingering illness. I don't think I could bear watching him suffer."

"I'm glad he went with his loved ones close, even if he went in his sleep. Was his health very bad before last week?" Emmett asked.

"After he got sick the first time, he was weaker and slower, but he seemed all right. Mother told me on the train that he didn't, um, couldn't function... as a man. I had no idea. She said he didn't feel like he was a real man after that."

"That's tough on a man, especially one who's still as young as your father was."

"There's more to being a man than just that, you know."

"Oh, Lacy, not to most men. I know what you mean, but

trust me, having that happen would be a serious blow to a man so young."

"GOOD AFTERNOON," the man behind the hotel counter said.

"Good afternoon, can you tell me if Deacon and Tillie Snow are in?"

The man turned to the key slots on the wall. "Yes, sir, I believe they are."

"Could you send someone to tell them the Burkes are here, please? We'll be in your bar over there."

"Yes, sir, we'll tell them right now." He whistled to a bell-hop, who ran up the stairs.

Emmett nodded to the man and guided Lacy to a quiet corner table in the bar.

When the Snows arrived, Emmett stood to welcome them.

"Our plans have changed since we arrived. We found Lacy's father to be quite ill, and he passed away early this morning."

"Oh, I'm so sorry, Lacy. Can we do anything for you? We'll be happy to, anything you or your mother need," Tillie offered.

"Yes, we do need something. First, I need to explain everything that led up to the predicament I'm in now, so you'll have all the background information. We want to hire you for some detective work here in town. Are you available to do that?"

Deacon answered, "Of course, we are." He took a pad of paper out of the inside pocket of his jacket and prepared to take notes.

Lacy explained everything and left nothing out. She told them about Carl, Alan, Heather, Harold, Gerald, the Nixons, and the deputy. Emmett explained his suspicions about the true relationship between Carl and Alan, but that he wasn't sure. They explained about Deputy Faust and how he had wanted to court Lacy and tried to accuse her and how Emmett had decked him once because he slapped a woman. They explained about the doctor's assertion that the Nixons had been murdered slowly and painfully with arsenic.

Deacon asked Lacy if she knew any places where Carl and Alan liked to go, such as bars or gentlemen's clubs, or even restaurants. There were a few other questions and she answered to the best of her knowledge.

The Snows promised to get started that afternoon.

THE HOUSE WAS full of people when they got back. The pastor and his wife were there, as was the doctor, several members of their church and a neighbor or two. Food trays and dishes were all over the countertops. George's body had already been moved to the funeral home.

The funeral was scheduled for two days later, on Thursday at noon.

"Mother, I know you didn't sleep last night. You look so tired. Why don't you go lie down? We'll take care of things in here and see to the guests."

"I'll be all right, dear. I'd like to thank all the callers myself."

The neighbors who overheard took the hint and made their exit. Some of the church members did, but it took a while longer for the pastor and his wife to leave. By late afternoon, all the visitors were gone, and Amelia decided she could lie down for a nap.

Emmett and Lacy were busy cleaning up after the guests when they heard a knock at the door. Lacy went to the parlor to answer it, fully prepared to ask any mourners to come back the next day when her mother felt better. But it wasn't a mourner.

"Deputy," Lacy said, a bit surprised to see him.

"Miss Lacy," he said, standing so straight that he appeared to be trying to make himself look taller, the way a small child might.

Emmett walked into the room. "It's Mrs. Lacy now," he said. "She's married to me."

The deputy's expression showed surprise and confusion. "Burke. I thought we were rid of you."

"Yet here I am. How can we help you this evening?"

"I've come to question Lacy... Mrs. Burke. I have reason to believe she played a part in the murder of Carl Nixon and the murders of his parents." The deputy stuck out his chin and Lacy thought he was trying to look official.

"Deputy, you've already questioned me about Carl's death. I wasn't there. I was home all morning and a houseful of people saw me. As for Mr. and Mrs. Nixon, I've never even been in their house."

"That's what you say," he said accusingly.

"That's what all the people you questioned said, too. You know as well as I do that Lacy is no more guilty of those deaths than I am. And before you ask, I didn't even know Lacy then." He stepped closer to the deputy to look more intimidating. "I'll thank you to leave my wife alone and do your job. Question the people, and this time, check their stories. Somewhere out there, somebody has information you need. Find it. You've got at least one murderer out there getting away. And make it clear to people that Lacy is not under suspicion."

"I can't do that until the investigation is over."

Emmett took another step toward the man. "Yes, you can."

"Well," the deputy said hotly. "Well. This isn't over until I say it is."

Emmett took another step, getting closer than another person usually would stand. His voice was soft but carried a menacing timbre. "Then you'd better say it is."

Deputy Faust turned on his heels and huffed back to his horse.

When the door closed again, Lacy smiled at Emmett. "Thank you for defending my honor."

"It was my pleasure." He chuckled. "And my duty, but in this case, it was definitely a distinct pleasure."

THE DAYS PASSED by in a blur for Lacy and her mother. There was a touching funeral for George, and Amelia was grateful the church was overflowing. It was comforting that so many people thought so highly of him, so much so that the thought made it easier for her to say goodbye to him.

She was numbed by the number of things she now had to take care of. First, there were George's personal belongings. They chose a very few items that meant a lot to George and kept them, but they gave away everything else to the church's charity drive.

As they laboriously went through the accounting paperwork for the store, Amelia came to the unmistakable conclusion that she did indeed want to move to Big Rock and be near her daughter. If Emmett and Lacy should have children, she wanted to be close to them. That decision dictated what they did with everything else.

There were some household items Amelia wanted to keep, everything from kitchen items to larger furniture. To make things easier and more manageable, they crated things, and when they thought they had a wagonload, they shipped it. Emmett wired Gann with each shipment and told him when the crates would arrive on the stage, and Gann would take them and store them in the empty bedrooms of Emmett and Lacy's house.

The decision to sell the store and the house was much easier for Amelia than she thought it would be. As much as she liked the idea of Gann's to have a steady income, she wanted to sever her ties to Laramie and completely start over. She would receive a good amount of money for both of them, and she should be set. Even though Emmett had wealth and promised to take care of her, she didn't want to be financially dependent on him unless she absolutely had to be. Thank goodness Emmett was there to help her deal with the sales.

One afternoon, when Emmett was away taking care of some banking business, mother and daughter sat down to glasses of lemonade after a morning of crating Amelia's books and some sewing supplies. It was a refreshing and well-deserved break.

"It's going to be nice having you there with us, Mother. I'm glad you decided to come."

"I didn't let you know how much I missed you those days you were away. It was breaking my heart not to have you here every day. The only thing I'm uncomfortable with is that I'll be in your home, underfoot. No house can survive two mistresses. It's your home, and I won't interfere with the way you run it. I'll do at least my share of the work."

"I missed you, too. And it's a very big house, Mother. I don't think you could possibly be underfoot that much. It's so big, there might even be days when you don't see us." That wasn't likely, but she was making a point.

"I did enjoy the house, I have to admit. Tell me something, though. That night when you yelled out *'fuck me'*... well, are you always that loud? I may have to fashion some earplugs."

Lacy let out an anguished cry and dropped her face to cover it with her hands.

Amelia burst out in a belly laugh and it felt good to her after all the crying she'd done in the last few days. "I didn't mean to embarrass you, sweetheart. I just wanted to tease you a little bit. I'm a woman, too, you know. I'm thrilled you've found your happiness." She lowered her voice. "And feel free to scream *fuck me* several times a day if you like. Or more specifically, if Emmett likes. You will need his participation after all."

Lacy dropped her face to the table and groaned.

NINE

They were almost finished with supper when Emmett had an idea.

"Amelia, I'm embarrassed I didn't think about this sooner. You've had your own home for so long, you might not be quite as happy living in our house. We have lots of land. Gann and I can build a house for you. If you ever decide to remarry, your new husband would be welcome to live there, too, if he doesn't already have a place of his own."

Amelia looked at her daughter. "Oh, you told him I overheard you two. I was just kidding with you, sweetheart. Really, Emmett, I don't need another house because of it. It's nothing, really."

Emmett looked confused. "Overheard what?"

Lacy closed her eyes in embarrassment and discomfort. "Emmett, she heard me yell *fuck me* that night you tied me up."

"You tied her up?" Amelia asked, her eyes wide. "We never did that."

"I didn't hurt her," he assured her.

Amelia stifled a laugh. "I could tell."

Lacy looked at Emmett. "I'm glad she wasn't on the train with us."

"Oh, I wish I'd never said anything about it. I didn't mean to make anyone uncomfortable. Listen, about building a house for me. It really isn't necessary. Besides, what if you build the house, then I remarry and move into his house? What would you do with an empty house on your land?"

Emmett shrugged. "I guess we'd have a guest house. Tell you what. We won't start on your house immediately. You can stay for a couple of months and see what you think. But the offer to build you a house stands."

Amelia smiled at him fondly. "Thank you, Emmett."

———

EMMETT ANSWERED the knock at the door.

"Mr. Emmett Burke?"

"Yes."

"A message for you from Mr. Hogan at First Bank of Laramie." He handed Emmett the envelope.

"Thank you," Emmett said as he handed the courier a coin. He walked back into the kitchen and sat at the table where Amelia and Lacy were sitting. He pulled out the note and read it.

"Ah, good news. Mr. Hogan says he has a potential buyer for the store. He wants to let the man tour it tomorrow. Hogan says if there's anything in the store you'd like to keep, it would be best to get it out today." He looked up at Amelia. "I agree with him. When he makes an offer, he'll expect everything he saw to be his. Is there anything you want to get?

"Let's go take a look. The dry goods I have are a little better quality than what I saw at the mercantile in Big Rock, so I'd like to take Lacy and pick the ones we want to keep. There might be other things, too."

"Why did you go to First Bank? That's not where Mother and Father do their banking."

"I still have a sizable account there. He sold my house when I moved and did a good job. Can you be ready in a few minutes? I'll go hook up the wagon in case you find a few things to bring back."

DEACON AND TILLIE SNOW sat at the kitchen table with Lacy, Amelia, and Emmett.

"We've learned about some of the suspects, and from what we can tell, the sheriff's office hasn't been as busy trying to solve these crimes. We can't figure out why, but we want to. Deputy Faust still wants to blame you, but since there's no evidence, he's had to give up official pursuit. But that doesn't keep him from telling his cronies you're getting away with murder."

"What have you been able to find out?" Lacy asked as she poured them more coffee.

"Gerald Nixon is of great interest. Even his close friends find his behavior erratic and even questionable. He's piled up gambling debts in both Laramie and Cheyenne. He certainly had the opportunity to poison his parents. He also had the opportunity to shoot his brother Carl; we can't alibi him for that time. Obviously his motive, if he did the acts, was to collect the inheritance from his parents. That would have gone a long way to pay off his debts. His relationship with his brother is a curious one. His drinking buddies say he was both jealous of Carl and loved him. He spoke derisively of him but wasn't specific about his complaint with Carl."

"Are you saying you suspect he killed Carl?" Lacy asked.

"That's where it gets murkier," Deacon said. "I talked to the men who came to get Carl's body when he was shot. Did you know he was shot twice?"

"No," Emmett said.

"He was. The men said the bullet holes, both in the back, didn't look the same, as you would expect them to. One had powder burns around the hole in the clothing that prove he was shot at close range. But the other bullet hole didn't, and it looked like a larger hole. There was blood spattered on the wall. But there was also a big puddle of blood under him on the floor. The man from the undertaker's office who took the body said it didn't look like the bullets were fired at the same time. The blood under him was fresher."

"Are you thinking there were two shooters? Two different guns?" Emmett asked.

"That, or the same person hung around a while after shooting him the first time and shot him again."

"Why would he hang around?" Amelia asked. "If I shot someone, the first thing I'd want to do is get out of there."

Deacon shrugged. "Could have been trying to hide his tracks; we can only speculate at this point."

"But it's possible the shooter shot Carl, then, say, cleaned up after himself in the house, then perhaps he saw that Carl wasn't dead and shot him again," Lacy said.

"It's possible. But one bullet hole did look bigger, and how likely is it that the shooter would have shot him with two different guns?" Deacon countered.

"We assumed Carl was getting ready for the wedding when he was shot. Do you know what he was wearing when he was shot? If it wasn't his good suit, it might have been much earlier when he was shot the first time," Lacy offered.

Deacon wrote some notes on his pad. "Excellent point, Lacy. I'll check."

"Did you find out anything about Heather and Harold Matthews?"

"Nothing at all. Heather was at your wedding, too, so she'd have had to have an accomplice. Harold was out of town. Besides, neither of them had a motive. There was no scandal around them. I don't believe either of them were involved at all."

"I never thought so, either," Lacy said. "What did you find out about Alan? He was Carl's best friend, so surely he would know if Carl had any enemies."

Deacon took a deep breath. "Yes, Alan... he and Carl were close. There have been hints that they were lovers."

Lacy gasped. "Well, what does that mean as far as whether or not he could have killed Carl or Carl's parents?"

"We're still investigating. That isn't clear yet. And we haven't been able to find him. Do you have any idea where he might be?"

"I don't. I don't even know where he lives," Lacy answered.

"We found his home, but he hasn't been there."

———

THAT NIGHT as they lay in Lacy's bed in her childhood home, Emmett pulled her close. "It's been a few days since I made you shout *fuck me*. I surely would like to hear it again." He teased her nipples.

"Yes, it has. How about if I don't yell out those particular words? How about if I don't yell out at all so I don't have to worry about being embarrassed?"

"Are you saying I should gag you?"

Lacy laughed. "No. But maybe you could put your hand across my mouth when the time comes."

"I could do that." Emmett pulled up her nightgown and put

his hand between her legs. "Do you think you could just not shout?"

"I might be able to do it if you don't tease me so much, if you don't keep me right at the edge for so long. I think that's what does it."

"We can try that. Might take some of the fun out of it, but we can try."

"I think it'll still be fun." She put her hand on him under the covers and chuckled. "Do you just, you know, stay in that condition?"

He laughed. "Have some mercy, woman. I was used to having you three or four times a day until we came out here."

"Kiss me. Kiss me like you mean it. I'll make you happy. And when you make me happy, I promise to be quiet."

AT BREAKFAST THE NEXT MORNING, Emmett brought up the subject of the sale of the house.

"If we got a solid offer on the store, the next step is putting the house up for sale. Amelia, that's a big step for you. When do you think you might be ready?"

"Last night, I lay in bed thinking about that very thing. To tell you the truth, it's getting harder and harder to sleep in the bed I shared with George. At first it made me feel close to him. Now it's a reminder that I can't cling to the past. I need to move on, Emmett. Soon."

"All right. How much more is there that we need to ship to Big Rock?"

"Just the fabric bolts I got yesterday. Since it's not much, can't they just go with us?"

"Yes, they can," he said. "I'll tell Hogan you're ready to sell the house. I already mentioned it, so he's been expecting the word. The livery will buy the horses if you want. I don't want to leave live animals here."

"Let's give them to the pastor. If they can't use them, they'll know of someone who can."

"All right. There's no reason why we can't take the train day after tomorrow. Is there?"

"Sounds good to me," Lacy said.

"It sounds horribly quick and at the same time, not quick enough," Amelia said. "But I'll be ready."

They split the rest of the day between packing and cleaning the house to ready it for the sale. She'd shipped so many of her things, they had to rearrange the items that were left to make it look like a home. Amelia commented about how much larger it looked with so much less furniture. "Let that be a lesson to me. Don't buy things you don't need, and you'll have more room."

Emmett sent Gann one last wire to let him know when to meet them at the stage. He also visited Mr. Hogan at the bank in the afternoon to let him know they were ready to leave and he could sell the house. The last errand he ran was to the Belmont to see the Snows.

"Lacy's mother is ready to leave for Big Rock. We're ready to get back home, too. Is there any possibility you two could take us to the train station Saturday morning?"

"Of course, we can," Deacon said.

Emmett laughed. "Well, it's more than just that, actually. I need to you make a delivery for me after we leave. I'll have the wagon packed and we'll come get you and Tillie here, then head for the train station. After you drop us off, I need you to take the wagon back to the house and unhook the horses. Amelia wants to give the team to her pastor, so I need you to take them to him. We'll sell the wagon and tack with the house."

"We can do that. Be happy to."

"Tell you what—let's leave by eight-fifteen and we'll have

time to go out for breakfast before we have to catch the train. That way, we won't have to make breakfast and clean up afterwards."

THE NEXT DAY, they did a little more tidying and last touches on the house before Emmett drove them around. Amelia wanted to see some of her best friends to say goodbye and let them know how to write to her.

"Emmett, will you drive by the blacksmith shop where you worked when you were here? I want to see it."

"Sure, I can do that. It's on the other side of town, just a block or two from that restaurant where I decked Deputy Faust. We can have supper there if you like."

"Good. I'm starting to get hungry," Amelia said.

They drove by the smithy and Emmett pointed out a few things about the street. "You notice it's a good location by the proximity to the livery stable. The stagecoach office is around the corner. It's a good customer, too."

"The original owner picked a good place," Amelia said.

Emmett chuckled. "That would be me. Business was so good, I had to hire another blacksmith. He bought the business from me when I left."

"Do you want to stop and talk to him?" Lacy asked.

"Looks like he's with a customer now. Maybe we'll stop on our way out of Rockwell's."

They drove on a little farther to the restaurant. Emmett greeted the hostess, who remembered him. It didn't surprise Lacy; women tended to remember Emmett. If this one had been younger, she might have had twinges of jealousy.

They were seated in a more secluded area, out of the way of traffic, enjoying an appetizer when Lacy saw him. "Oh no, what's that French word for when it feels like something's happened before? *Déjà vu*? Emmett, this may be *déjà vu* for you."

"What is it?" he asked.

"Deputy Faust just walked in, with a woman. He'd better not slap this one, or we'll both jump on him."

"No, darlin'. If anything happens, you let me take care of it. I won't have you laying into someone, especially in public. It's possible he'll be gentleman." Emmett sighed. "Not likely, but it's possible."

Dinner was a little more subdued than it might have been if the deputy hadn't shown up. All three of them found themselves trying to listen more intently. They still enjoyed dinner, though, including a dessert of peach cobbler with cream.

Emmett picked up their bill and leaned over to speak quietly. "There's no way to get out of here without passing their table. I don't want either of you talking to him. Nod if you'd like to, but don't engage him. I want to ask him what they've found out about the case because it's my last chance to confront him before we leave. Understand?"

Both of the ladies nodded.

When they stood up, Emmett took Lacy by the elbow and Amelia walked behind them. The deputy saw them approach and visibly bristled.

"Good evening, Deputy," Emmett said. "We leave tomorrow to go back home, and I was wondering if you could tell me what you've been able to find out about Carl Nixon's murder and the poisoning of his parents."

"It's an ongoing investigation," he said, then he picked up his fork again as if to dismiss them.

"That's encouraging; at least you haven't given up."

"Of course, I haven't given up. We both know your wife is

guilty; we just can't come up with the evidence. I'll eventually find it."

"You contemptible weasel," Lacy said as she picked up the man's water and threw it on his chest. "You know darn well I did nothing wrong."

"You saw that!" the deputy said to the woman across the table from him. "That was assault."

Emmett pushed Lacy out of the way. "That was an accident. But I'm seriously considering assaulting you myself. Have you even looked at other suspects? Gerald Nixon? Alan Huntsman? Both of them had opportunity and motive, whereas my wife didn't."

"As the investigator, I'll be the judge of that."

"The judge. You've given me a good idea. You do your job, or I'll go to the judge with the information we've already put together. You know if he thinks you aren't doing your job, he'll call in the US Marshals Service. Think how embarrassing that would be for you."

"You'd better leave now, Burke. You're making me angry."

Emmett stood firmly and put his hands on his hips. "So angry, you'll slap me like you slapped that woman the night I knocked you out for it? I'll just do it again." He turned to the woman who had come in with the deputy. "Ma'am, I've witnessed the deputy hitting a young woman in this very restaurant. I urge you not to spend time with him."

She looked frightened and glanced at Faust. "He is quick to anger. I've noticed that."

Emmett held out his hand. "Come on, ma'am, we'll take you home. I imagine he's angry now."

The young woman picked up her reticule and took Emmett's hand.

"You'd better stay here with me, Marlene, if you know

what's good for you," the deputy spat, spittle flying across the table.

"He won't lay a hand on you, Marlene," Emmett said calmly as he looked directly at Faust. "He knows what I'll do if he does."

Amelia put her arm around Marlene and they hastily made their exit.

"I should thank you for rescuing me. I intended to tell him tonight that I wouldn't see him anymore."

"Then it's a good thing we were there," Emmett said. "You'd have been in danger if you'd done that."

They took Marlene home, but not before Emmett stopped at a bakery and purchased some specialty breads and meat pies since Marlene hadn't gotten a chance to eat supper.

TEN

Over breakfast the next morning, at a diner near the train station, Emmett told Deacon and Tillie about the encounter with the deputy the night before.

"I can't believe that man won't let go of Lacy as a suspect. It's irrational," Tillie said.

"Some men just hold a grudge," Amelia said.

"Yes," Tillie responded, "but logically, the grudge should be against Lacy's father, not Lacy."

"Maybe Lacy represents her father, or the whole incident, in his mind. After all, it was Lacy he wanted," Deacon said.

"Perhaps."

"Anyway, we got a lead on where Alan's been since Carl's funeral. He has a cousin in the Mount Morgan area, and he's believed to be there. It's about an hour's ride from here. We're going there today, once we get the horses delivered to the pastor."

"Wire me when you learn something. Well, wait until Tuesday morning, and I'll check the telegraph office when we get to town," Emmett said.

"Will do."

AFTER THE SUPPER stop that evening, Amelia said her goodnights and told the young couple she'd see them in the morning. Lacy kissed her goodnight and then she and Emmett went to their own unit in the Pullman car.

Lacy looked forward to seducing her husband because she knew the train made so much noise that with only a little effort on her part, she wouldn't be so loud her mother would hear. She selected one of her most revealing nighties and disappeared into the tiny water closet to freshen up and change.

When she emerged, she found Emmett sitting on the bed. The paddle was in his hand.

"Are we going to play this game again?" she asked with a grin.

"No game this time, darlin'. I'm serious."

Lacy searched his face and found no hint of humor or jest. She backed up. "Are you serious?"

"I am." His voice was calm but didn't invite argument.

"Why? What did I do?"

"Last night at the restaurant, I told you and your mother not to say anything to Faust and not to engage him. Do you remember that?"

She thought back. "Yes." It was a quiet and tentative *yes*.

"And what did you do?"

She closed her eyes, not wanting to remember. "I threw his water on him and called him a weasel." Her shoulders drooped.

"Why do you think I told you not to speak to him?"

Lacy looked away, not wanting to answer. "You knew how dangerous he can be," she said.

"That's exactly right. I even told you before how he'd assaulted a woman. You knew he could fly off the handle in an instant. Yet you chose to disobey me."

"B-but—"

"I'm listening. Do you have an excuse? A reason?"

"He accused me again, and it made me angry."

"I told you I'd handle him, didn't I?"

"Yes."

"Can you think of a good reason I shouldn't use this paddle on you?"

Lacy wanted to shrink into the floor. "You could believe me when I say I'm sorry and I won't do it again."

"I could. Put yourself in my place. Would you believe you and let it go at that?"

"Probably not."

"I don't tell you to do many things, or not to do things. I would only do it when there's a good reason, and in this case, it was for your safety. You could have been hurt. When I specifically tell you something like that, I don't want to be ignored. I will not be ignored, Lacy. Do you understand what I'm telling you? You mean far too much to me for me to just let it go when you put yourself in danger. Do you understand?"

"Yes." It was a whisper.

"Then you agree with me that you deserve this."

Lacy wracked her brain trying to think of a reason why she shouldn't agree.

"I'm waiting for an answer. Do you agree you deserve this?"

She knew there was no escaping it. "Yes. I mean, I don't want it, but I can see your point. But please, Emmett, not too hard. I don't want Mother to know."

"She already knows."

"You told her?" She looked at him incredulously.

"She came to me and told me you deserved it. I had already made the decision, though, so she didn't influence me. This is all my doing; you can't blame her. Now come on. Over my lap." He patted his knee.

Her mouth dried up and her legs felt glued to the spot.

"Come on, darlin'. Don't make it worse."

He helped her over his left knee, her upper body on the bed. "Grab that pillow and hold it. It may help you stay put."

"How bad will it be?"

"Bad enough to hurt. When was the last time you were punished like this?"

"It's been years. Maybe four or five years."

"Did your father or mother do it?"

"Usually Father. He used his belt," she said, and the memory of the pain came back. What had hurt more, though, was knowing she'd behaved badly enough to disappoint her parents.

"I reckon I'll use a belt sometimes in the future. Not enough room to swing one on this train."

"Do you plan to do this... often?"

He gave a hollow laugh. "That's up to you. I hadn't planned to have to do this tonight." Emmett pulled her gown up to her back and began to rub her bottom. "I'd rather be doing something else entirely."

"I'm sorry, Emmett, I really am. Will you go ahead and do what you have to? I'd like to get it over with."

He pulled back the paddle and let her have it.

She cried out, trying not to be too loud. "How many are you going to give me?"

"I don't honestly know, darlin'. I guess I'll stop when I think it's done some good." He swung again and hit the other cheek, then he paused. "You should see this. Your bottom says *Lacy Obey*."

"Then can we stop now?"

He laughed for real. "I think you've forgotten what a paddlin' should feel like. We aren't there yet."

She steeled herself and hugged the pillow. *Splat!* Then

another. Then another. The paddle was long enough to have a little carryover, but he alternated his aim between the two orbs and kept swinging.

Her lower legs jerked and kicked, and he warned her to try to be still and take her medicine. Emmett was the strongest man she'd ever met, and her mind reeled over how bad this paddling could be if he used even half his strength. She would have deep, painful bruises. With each lick, she cried into the pillow, trying to keep quiet.

He paused and rubbed her red bottom. "It's nice and dark pink, darlin'."

She hoped that meant he was stopping.

It didn't.

"Hold tight now; these are going to hurt."

You mean those didn't?

She felt the paddle *splat* across the top of her right thigh. Lacy raised her head from the pillow and yelled. "Please, no, no, not there," she begged.

He aimed for her left thigh, and she cried out again. Her right fist beat the bedspread. Then he paused again and rubbed all over the redness.

"Emmett, please no more on my legs. I don't think I can take it."

"I think you can take as much as I want to give, but I'll stop. I only wanted to put the words there where I can see them. Spread your legs some, darlin'."

She gasped and leaned up on her arms. "You aren't going to paddle me there, are you?"

"No, darlin', the paddling's over."

Lacy's relief was apparent in her sigh. She parted her legs.

Emmett rubbed all over her bottom again, not too hard, but enough to ignite the tender skin. He rubbed down on her thighs and made his way to the inside of them, then rubbed back up on her bottom. The heat she felt turned into a warm glow under his touch. He massaged down to her thighs again, and this time, he insinuated his hand into her slit.

Lacy was dismayed to realize she'd become wet while he rubbed her. It happened when he rubbed her, right? And not during the paddling? Her dismay turned into mortification.

He gently pushed two fingers inside her and moved them in and out.

Lacy was aroused and confused. *How is this happening now? I never reacted like this when Father punished me. Is there something wrong with me?*

Emmett pulled out his sopping wet fingers and plunged his middle one into her little brown rosette. She cried out in surprise and protest.

"Why are you doing that?"

"Because you don't like it yet."

"Yet?"

"Maybe one day you will. Some women do. But right now, I can punctuate this paddlin' with something to make it more memorable for you."

"I promise I'll remember it. You can stop that now."

Instead of stopping, he thrust his finger in and out. She realized right away that he was simulating sex back there.

"There. Are you going to obey me from now on?"

"I will."

"I'm going to hold you to that. It'll be worse if I have to do this again. Understand?"

She sighed. "Yes."

He patted her backside. "Hop up. I'll go wash my hands." The implication embarrassed her, and she couldn't meet his eyes as she got up. He came back from the water closet naked and crawled into bed beside her. On his back, arms under his pillow, he didn't make a move toward her.

"You're not, I mean, are we not—"

He cut off her words. "If you want something from me, take it."

Lacy had to think for a moment about what he meant. When she realized what it was, she scrambled to her knees and took his semi-hardness into her mouth.

He responded with a stiffening member and moans, pulling her hair out of the way so he could watch her mouth as that part of him disappeared into it. "I told you to take what you want. While I love what you're doing, if you want your own satisfaction, you should probably concentrate on that."

She looked up, and again, it took a few seconds to figure out what he meant. She straddled him and lowered herself down on his hard length.

His hands stayed under his head and she wished to goodness he'd reach up and fondle her. He didn't. But he watched intently. She used her knees to let herself rise and fall. She developed a rhythm and closed her eyes to feel the sensations. Her breasts bounced and Emmett's eyes focused on them. Her legs cramped with the effort and she started moving in a forward and backward motion, reminiscent of the way he thrust into her. It was a different sensation than up and down, and although both felt wonderful, it still wasn't getting her there.

She reached up to her breasts and cupped them, then zeroed in on her own nipples. She rolled and pinched and tweaked and twisted, the way Emmett did. It wasn't the same as when he did it, but it still took her closer.

She opened her eyes to find his locked on hers. Lacy hoped the need in her eyes would invite him to touch her, but he still lay there with his arms under his head. She reached her right hand down to her little pearl and rubbed around it in a circular motion, ending up in a sideways motion. Her breath quickened, and her perspiration fell in droplets on him. She went back to that up and down motion, ignoring the ache in her thighs. She was almost there.

Lacy realized he was bucking up to meet her, and that's when she felt herself letting go. His arms jerked out beside him to give him some leverage and he thrust harder and harder until they both collapsed, spent both physically and emotionally.

———

"YOU DESERVED THAT LAST NIGHT, you know," Amelia said over her breakfast plate. Emmett had gone for seconds.

"You heard it?" Lacy was embarrassed.

"Not really. The train makes a lot of noise. I heard muffled sounds, but if I hadn't already known what was going to happen, I wouldn't have been able to tell." Amelia's face softened. "You could have been hurt by that deputy. From what I can tell, he's no better behaved than a mad dog."

"Still, a paddling? I'm a married woman, after all. I should be able to make some choices by myself."

"And the most important choice you can make is to honor your husband. Yours is a fine man and he deserves your respect." Amelia looked at her pointedly. "And it doesn't matter how old you are. Husbands have the right to make you mind them. Some would argue they have the duty to do so."

"You're thirty-eight years old, Mother. Thirty-eight. Don't you think that's old enough for you to make up your own mind and make your own choices?"

Amelia put her napkin down and took Lacy's hand. "Sweetheart, this is how the world is. There are men and there are women, and they aren't the same. We wouldn't want them to be the same. Your father exercised his duty with me and made me straighten up and fly right. He was right to do it. I don't believe I'd have the regard for him that I have if he'd let me get away with all those things."

"Will you still feel that way if you remarry?"

"I'm sure I will. I wouldn't marry a man I didn't trust to lead me and our family. You really aren't angry with Emmett for last night, are you?"

Lacy sighed. "No. We made up, sort of."

Amelia chuckled. "That's not making up. I think of it as God's little gift to compensate for a busted and burnt backside. It helps to reestablish the relationship. Don't you think?"

"I suppose so."

"That's how it should work. Once he's taken you to task, it's over. Debt paid. Tell me, how was he this morning?"

Lacy smiled. "Back to normal, in a magnificent fashion."

Emmett returned then with a filled plate and Amelia didn't get to respond. "Have I missed out on the conversation?" he asked.

Amelia answered, "No, we were just talking about the journey." It wasn't technically a lie. She didn't say what journey.

"I heard the conductor say we're ahead of schedule. Winds have been at our tail and the water stops went faster than usual."

"So we'll get to Rawlins in plenty of time, then. We won't have to rush to get to the stagecoach," Lacy said.

"Right. I want to get all our canteens filled and make sure we have some food on board with us. You know how uncomfortable stagecoaches are. They're downright miserable when you're hungry or thirsty."

ELEVEN

It was a pleasant trip from Laramie to Big Rock. Much of the talk was centered on where the best place might be to build a new house for Amelia and all the amenities they would add to it. Emmett made his mother-in-law feel like a most loved and welcome member of their new family. Lacy might have fallen in love with him just a little more, too.

Emmett had an enormous amount of land that spread from near the old silver mine to across the river, all the way to the outskirts of the other side of town. There were fields and forests, streams, hills and valleys, and according to Emmett, it was all beautiful.

"It might take some time to decide the best place for your house, so we can spend that time drawing up some plans you'll love. I want you to have everything you ever wanted, Amelia. Gann and I can build anything you want."

He'd been telling her that, but tears still came to her eyes when she realized he meant it.

"Oh, Emmett, you are such a blessing. I thank God for bringing you and Lacy together and letting me be a part of it."

Emmett leaned over and kissed Lacy on the cheek. "I thank

God for that, too. It's always been my dream to find the woman I love and settle down. Maybe we'll have some little ones come along soon. Who knows?"

Lacy wanted to speak up, but until she was sure, she chose to keep silent. She just smiled.

"Em, you know it's possible that Mother could remarry. Are you sure you're all right with another man moving onto your property, I mean, provided she doesn't move out of her house and into his home?"

"If I like the fellow, I won't mind," Emmett said. "I've thought about that. Amelia, I hope you understand that I'm probably going to be very protective of you if that time should come. I want to see you happy. If a man comes along who makes you happy and he passes muster with me, I'll cut out a good parcel of land your house sits on and give it you as a wedding gift."

"Oh, Emmett, that's far too generous! It might not even happen, you know. I could never expect you to do such a thing."

Emmett chuckled. "I fully imagine it will happen, Amelia. Look at you. You're a beautiful woman, still young at thirty-eight. I've known women who married late in life who didn't even begin their families until they were your age. I'm sure it'll happen. And when it does, we'll deal with it. I just wanted to let you know I've thought about it."

A few more tears made their way out of Amelia's eyes and down her cheek before she dabbed them away with a gloved hand.

EMMETT'S UNCLE GANN met them in town when the stage arrived. It was a happy reunion and they caught up on things over lunch at Mama Mary's Restaurant.

"Gann," Amelia said with sincere appreciation, "I can't tell you how much it means to me that you've been taking my things from the stage and transporting them to Emmett's house. That's a kindness that's just above and beyond what anyone should expect of another. I hope you'll let me return the favor by cooking a few meals for you, or something such as that. I don't think I could ever repay you for all that work."

"Nonsense," Gann said with a smile. "I'm happy to help out all I can."

Emmett laughed. "It's not like he has a job you kept him away from. There's no telling what kind of mischief you kept him from getting into."

"Still," Amelia said, "you must have spent as much time at Emmett's house as you did your own."

Gann gave her a big grin that brought out his dimples. "You might be right about that part," was all he said.

Amelia found herself grinning back at him, largely at his dimples. His grin with those dimples gave him such a young, handsome, roguish quality. He really wasn't old, she thought, probably about her age, maybe a little older. But he seemed so much younger and more vital than George had been. She realized Gann made her feel younger, too.

Emmett changed the subject. "Before we head home, I want to check at the telegraph office and see if I have any wires from Deacon Snow. I want to know if they've gotten any further with Carl's murder."

"What do they know so far?" Gann asked.

"Not much. That idiot Faust is only interested in blaming Lacy; he's got a personal vendetta and it's ridiculous. Deacon was going to track down Alan Huntsman, Carl's friend. We think they were, um, very close friends."

"Hmm," Gann mused. "Do you really think he'd have killed Carl if they were in their own relationship?"

"Well, husbands and wives kill each other. You can read about a new incident every time you pick up a newspaper. I don't know why they'd be any different," Emmett said. "Carl's brother Gerald is a strong suspect, too. Deacon's working on that angle."

"Well, what's that deputy and the sheriff's office looking into?"

"Damn near nothing," Emmett responded.

"I wonder if Alan and Gerald could have been in cahoots," Gann said.

Emmett looked at him and squinted a little bit. He hadn't considered that possibility.

EMMETT BOUNDED out of the telegraph office holding two envelopes. He gracefully jumped into the back of the wagon and settled in crosswise behind the seat that held Gann, Amelia, and Lacy.

"We got some great news, Amelia. The bank wired that you got a full-price offer on the store. I sent back a message for them to accept it and wire you the money here. They're working on advertising the house now. Here you go; here's the wire."

"Woohoo!" Gann hollered in celebration. "I believe you're now officially a rich widow."

"Oh, Mother, that's right," Lacy said. "You're going to have to be wary that some men might only want you for your money."

Amelia looked at her daughter with a little bit of good-natured indignation. "Are you saying that's all I have to offer? My money?"

Both of the men hooted, and Emmett clicked his tongue at his wife. "Dearie, you got yourself into that one."

Lacy shook her head, grinning. "No, no, I didn't mean it that way. I only meant that it's possible there are unscrupulous men out there on the prowl for a good woman they can take advantage of."

"Nice way to fix that flub, Lacy," Gann said with a chuckle. "I'm not sure you're out of the hole yet, but at least you stopped digging."

Lacy laughed. "Mother, on the ride back, let's keep our eyes peeled for pretty spots to build your house. Emmett can remind us where his land starts so we'll know where to look. Wait a minute, we might not have to build on Emmett's land. You'll have enough money to buy your own land once the property sales are final. You can get as close to town as you'd like if that's important to you."

Emmett agreed but added, "I'd rather you be closer to us, though."

"You had two envelopes, hon. What was the other message?" Lacy asked.

"It's from Deacon. He's updating me on the investigation."

"Good news?"

"I don't know. Perplexing news. The day we left, he and Tillie were going to try to track down Alan Huntsman, Carl's lover. They went to Mount Morgan and found him, all right. Found him dead, hanging from a ceiling rafter."

Lacy gasped. "Oh no! Poor Alan. Was it, I mean, did he..."

Emmett shook his head. "Faust is calling it a suicide, but Deacon said that would have been impossible."

"How so?" Gann asked.

"Don't know. Deacon didn't send any more details."

"Suppose it was murder," Amelia said. "Who would have wanted to kill him?"

"Good question," Emmett said. "Maybe Gerald? If he

suspected that Alan killed Carl, maybe he wanted to avenge his brother's death."

"Is he sure it was impossible to be suicide? That could make sense if he was grieving over the loss of Carl and didn't want to live without him," Lacy offered.

"I don't know," Gann said. "If I were given a choice of suicide by hanging or by gunshot, I'd choose the gun. Much quicker and easier. Why would a man with a gun kill himself by hanging?"

Amelia responded. "Why would a killer hang a man when he could just shoot him? We can probably assume whoever hanged him had a gun. Most men do."

"I don't think I could ever be a lawman or a detective," Lacy said. "You get one question answered, and a dozen more pop up."

Emmett agreed.

THEY HAD RIDDEN a few minutes in silence when Lacy gently elbowed her mother to get her attention. "Mother, look, this is a pretty spot. I can imagine a house built over there in front of those trees. They'd make a nice backdrop."

"It is pretty. It's all pretty out here. But it might be too early to decide on a location. We have all the time in the world."

Lacy laughed. "I'm not asking Emmett to pick up a shovel just yet, I'm just looking at pretty locations along the way."

"All right, then," Amelia said, grinning. "I have to agree, it's a beautiful spot."

"There's a spot just up ahead I like a lot," Emmett said. "There's a bend in the road that would be a good setting for a house."

"Oh, I know where you're talking about. That would be a

good place. A house would be pretty on either side of the bend," Lacy agreed.

When they neared it, Gann slowed the wagon to a near stop. He stopped it completely when they were in the sharpest point of the bend, which wasn't really sharp at all.

"All right, now that I'm here, I think the house would be best on this side. It would really look prominent situated on the inside of the bend. I can just imagine it right there, and I can see flower beds all across the front. What do you think, Mother?"

"It is beautiful."

Gann entered the conversation. "Where would you want the barn?"

"The barn?" Amelia asked. "Oh, I suppose I will have to have a horse or two. I won't be in the city anymore. I hadn't thought about that. George always took care of our horses. I'll have to learn how to do that." A frown overtook her face.

"Mother, you managed a thriving business and raised a daughter. I can't imagine that taking care of horses will be harder than either one of those."

That brought a few chuckles from the men.

"Mother!" Lacy said with enthusiasm. "Emmett said I can have chickens. He and Gann have drawn up some plans already. You should get some chickens, too."

"Let's not go overboard, dear. We're already talking about a house and a barn. Let's not add a chicken coop just yet. I think that one could wait."

"What about a garden?" Gann asked. "Would you like a vegetable patch?"

"Oh, my," Amelia said. "I never had one of those, either. I think we can hold off on that one, too."

"We'll have to keep it in mind, just in case. We'll want to make sure it's near a water source."

"So many things to think about!" Amelia said, shaking her head at the thought of making all the decisions.

When they reached the house, Gann pulled up as close to the front steps as he could. He and Emmett began handing off items and placing them on the porch to be taken in later in a more orderly fashion.

Lacy cocked her head, listening. "What's that... is that... are those chickens I hear?"

A big broad grin broke out across Gann's face and his dimples never looked so big or made him look so impish. Lacy ran around to the back of the house to find the most unusual coop she'd ever seen. The others followed her.

The architecture mimicked the house, even down to an oversized door with handmade metal hinges. Even Emmett was impressed with Gann's attention to detail, but he still laughed in amusement over the grandest chicken coop he'd ever seen.

Lacy was almost overcome. She jumped and whooped and hollered and finally ran to Gann and gave him a big hug and kiss on the cheek. "I love it, Gann! I can't believe you did all this while we were gone. You are the sweetest, most thoughtful thing." She kissed his cheek again. "Thank you so much for this."

"Aw," he said, almost embarrassed at her reaction. "I wanted to give you a wedding gift, and this was something I knew you wanted. I'm glad you like it."

Emmett expressed his thanks, too, and again complimented the workmanship.

"Just one thing, though," Lacy said. "I have no idea how to raise chickens. You'll have to teach me."

The men laughed and agreed to show her what to do.

LATER, when all their things had been brought in and many of Amelia's belongings had been put away or stored in unused rooms, she paused and realized how late it was.

"Lacy, why don't you and I head to the kitchen and see what we can put together for dinner? I imagine we'll need to go to the store tomorrow."

"No, no need, I don't think," Gann said. "I made a big pot of beef stew and went ahead and shopped for perishables so you wouldn't have to. I knew you'd be tired after traveling."

"Gann, I don't know what to say. Lacy may be right. You might just be the sweetest, most thoughtful thing."

He grinned at her and Amelia noticed the twinkle in his eye and the half-smile that made one dimple a little deeper than the other. The thought struck her that the gray hairs at his temple gave him an air of maturity, but that big smile and those dimples gave him a boyish look that he'd have forever.

"I'll go heat up the stew and fry up some corn cakes to go with it."

Gann followed her into the kitchen and lit a fire in the stove.

"EMMETT, I want to talk to you about something. Last Sunday, the church house was so full, all the young'uns had to sit on the floor. I don't think we can wait until the building fund has enough money before we build a new one," Gann said.

"What are your thoughts?" Emmett asked.

"Just like I mentioned before. Instead of expanding the current building like they're talking about, I'd like to see a whole new building go up. We can use the existing building for a dedicated schoolhouse. I know that'll be welcome; it's a pain right now to have to rearrange furniture in there before services."

"That's a good idea. Do you think there's room for a bigger structure where they are now?"

"I need to check it out. If there's not room, the lot across the road is available."

"Show me your plans."

Gann laughed. "So far, they're only in my head. I want to talk to Reverend Copperfield before drawing up anything. The way this town's growing, the sanctuary needs to be substantially larger. I've heard the pastor's wife talk about how she'd like Sunday School rooms. I figure one room for the little toots and another one for the bigger kids. Grownups could have their Sunday School in the sanctuary. I'd like for the pastor to have his own little office. He needs one. And a place for a choir up front. I want a choir."

"Goodness," Amelia said. "Sounds like you've thought about this quite a bit."

"I have," Gann agreed. "The biggest expenditure would be lumber and labor. I'd like to suggest that Emmett and I split the remaining costs, above what's in the building fund, provided the labor is donated by the men. I'll talk to Angus and Henry at the sawmill and see if they'll discount or contribute the lumber. I'll talk to the pastor tomorrow, but it might be helpful if you're at the business meeting when I present it to the men."

"I can do that," Emmett said.

Lacy tried her best to stifle a yawn but she couldn't hide it.

"I know you're all tired," Gann said as he smiled. "When we're done, I'll clean up in here and go on home so you can all go to bed."

"No, I'll help you while the ladies run hot baths. I'm sure that's what's on their minds."

Lacy blew her husband a kiss and winked at him.

TWELVE

Emmett spent the next few mornings showing the ladies how to take care of chickens and horses. It didn't take much time on the chickens, but he spent a lot of time with the horses and was pleased at how much both of them enjoyed it. Before too long, they were both proficient at grooming, saddling, riding, and how to keep them supplied with fresh hay when they weren't grazing on grass.

"Just think how much fun it'll be to take horseback rides around the ranch," Lacy said, and Amelia agreed.

"Here's something I want you to do. If you have any problems, any problems at all and need me or Gann, shoot three times. We'll always come in a hurry if we hear three shots."

"That could be a problem, hon," Lacy said.

"Why?"

"I don't know how to shoot," she said.

"I don't have a gun," Amelia said.

Emmett slumped his shoulders in mock defeat and laughed. "All right, ladies. Shooting lessons begin tomorrow after breakfast. I'll get you both new guns this afternoon."

"Does that mean we're going into town?"

"It surely does. I want to stop by the telegraph office and check in at the blacksmith shop, too."

"Perfect. Mother and I can be shopping while you're taking care of business."

"I want to help pick out your guns. Let's do that first."

"Oh, if it's all right with you two, I think I'll stay here while you go," Amelia said.

"That's fine with us. Alone time is a good thing," Emmett said.

THE RIDE into town was enjoyable for Emmett and Lacy. It occurred to them that they hadn't been able to have much free-flowing, grown-up, marital type conversation regarding carnal things since Amelia moved in with them. It hadn't really limited their lovemaking, at least not any more than requiring them to limit it to their bedroom. But it had affected their day-in and day-out flirtatious conversation, and they missed it. They gleefully made up for lost time on the way into town.

Once in town, Emmett saw Angus Kelly, one of the owners of the sawmill, walking along the sidewalk. He pulled the wagon to a stop and called to Angus. Emmett stood to step down, but Angus stopped him.

"Doona get down, man, I'll be right there," he said in his Irish accent that sometimes amused the people in town. With his giant strides, he was beside the wagon in no time. "Afternoon, Miz Lacy," he said as he tipped his hat.

Emmett didn't give his wife time to respond. "I wondered if Gann had a chance yet to talk to you and Henry about lumber for the new church building. Did you discuss it?"

"Aye, we did. We're going to supply at least most of the lumber. We have a good supply laid by and a team of men out cutting all the standing dead timber they can find. We pinned Gann down and made him draw us a sketch of what they were thinking so we could estimate the amount we'll need. If we doona have enough, we'll have to resort to using fresh cut green."

"That's good to hear, but don't let the donation hurt your business. The building fund will probably have enough to pay a discounted price."

Angus chuckled. "Emmett, we all ken you and Gann pretty much *are* the building fund. But I'll keep that in mind. The business should be fine."

They said their goodbyes. Angus tipped his hat to Lacy again and resumed his walk down the street.

Emmett's eyes twinkled as he leaned down to Lacy and whispered, "Now if there's any man around here who might have a giant sequoia, it would be Angus."

"Emmett!" Lacy said, surprised and laughing.

"Well, the man's huge. He's three or four inches taller than I am, so it makes sense."

"Do men do this often? Think about other men's... trouser trees?"

Emmett nearly doubled over and actually giggled, whispering, "Trouser trees," under his breath. After his giggling fit, he added, "No, not other men's trouser trees. Just our own. We'd been talking about my mighty oak on the way into town, and then I saw Angus." Emmett laughed.

Lacy continued playfully, "You men. Always thinking about one thing."

"Are you going to tell me women never think of fleshly things? They never have lusty, lustful thoughts? Because if you try to tell me that, I won't believe you."

She grinned and lowered her head a little bit and then eyed him from under thick lashes. "All right, sometimes I do think about your mighty oak. I am fond of it, you know."

"I'm glad you admitted that. I'd be awfully discouraged if you didn't think about it. What exactly do you think about it?"

She laughed, deep and sultry. "I think about how I can make it go from an acorn to a mighty oak when I want to."

"Acorn? Oh, hell, woman! Acorn? At least you could say from a strong sapling to a mighty oak."

She cackled.

"All right, all right, tell me more things you think about."

"I think about kissing." She lowered her voice. "Your kisses make me melt, you know. I think of things we've done and some we haven't done."

"Now we're getting somewhere. What do you want to do that we haven't done?"

"I wonder if it would be possible to..." she turned to him and mouthed the word *fuck* since they were in town, "on the front porch swing. And I think I'd like to do it one clear night on a quilt under the stars."

"Ah, romantic. I'm seeing a pattern. You're an outdoor action girl and I never knew it."

"No, not particularly. It's just that the ranch is so much bigger than just the house."

"Well, one thing's for certain. We've got to get your mother's house built so we can do all those things without getting caught in the act. How about the barn? Ever thought about fucking in there?"

She shushed him. "Emmett! People might hear."

"Nah, they won't. Barn?"

"No, I haven't. Barns smell funny."

"We could try it on a horse sometime."

"Wouldn't that be dangerous?"

He grinned at her, stopped the wagon in front of the telegraph office, and jumped down. "I'll be right back. Haven't checked on wires in a few days."

Emmett came back outside a few minutes with a more pensive look on his face.

"News from Deacon?"

"Quite a bit. He and Tillie will arrive back in town the day after tomorrow. I'd like for us to meet their stage and take them to lunch so he can fill us in."

"What does the wire say?"

"A lot, and not enough. Deacon went to the judge and explained about Deputy Faust, and the judge agreed. He brought in a US Marshal and I recognized the name. Deacon's worked with him before. He turned everything on the case over to the marshal."

"Oh, my. I can imagine how well Faust took that," Lacy said.

"So can I. We're headed straight to the mercantile to get guns for you and Amelia and whatever else you need at the house. Then we're going straight home for shooting lessons. Before this day's done, you'll be an expert."

"You don't think he'd come here, do you?"

"Most likely not, but I'm taking no chances."

"MOTHER, WE'RE HOME!" Lacy called out as she entered the house. "Did you enjoy your afternoon?"

"I did, darling daughter, I surely did. I sat on the porch swing for a while, came in and wrote a couple of letters to friends back in Laramie, made a buttermilk pie, and was just thinking I might enjoy doing some sewing projects with you again like we used to do occasionally."

"Buttermilk pie, I haven't had one of those in ages," Emmett said with a big smile. "We need to leave you to your own devices more often."

"That would be fun," Lacy said. "But this afternoon, Emmett insists that we learn to use our new pistols. He said before we go to bed tonight, we'd be good enough to give Wild Bill Hickok a run for his money, that is, if he was still alive."

Amelia laughed. "I don't know about that, but I am eager to learn how to shoot. I imagine there are plenty of snakes and wild animals out here."

"There are," Emmett said. "Snakes in the summertime, mostly other animals in the winter when their food is scarcer. Most of the time, they'll shy away when they see a human, and there's no real danger and no need to shoot. But once in a while, well, you just need to be prepared."

"I've noticed you wear your gun belt anytime you're going to be outside for a while," Amelia said.

Emmett grinned. "Habit, but it's a good habit. After today, I'd like for you girls to take your pistols if you'll be outside for any length of time. There's no need if you're just going to collect eggs, but if you'll be out for a while or if you'll be going any farther away from the house, it would be a good idea to be armed."

"Should we have our own gun belts?" Lacy asked.

"Not a bad idea," Emmett said. "I think I have an old one in the barn you can try out."

"Or something with big pockets, like an apron," Amelia said, "that doesn't look quite so masculine."

Emmett laughed. "I will bow to fashion as you wish, but be sure to keep those pistols handy."

He set up a couple of wooden targets against the backdrop of the river and the forest behind it. Their guns were identical Colt Navy revolvers except that Lacy's had a more ornate grip than Amelia's plain woodgrain. Emmett commanded their attention as he showed them the parts of the gun and explained basic gun safety rules. He showed them how to load and unload them and promised to show them how to clean their guns that evening.

Emmett showed them individually how to hold the gun, line up the sights, and squeeze the trigger. He suggested they start close to the target, about twenty-five feet away, then move back as they become proficient at that distance.

Lacy shot first and hit her wooden target. She was elated and Emmett was proud.

"Nice job," he said with encouragement.

Amelia aimed at her target next. She took her time stabilizing her stance before she took aim and squeezed. Hers not only hit her target but also hit it in the circle Emmett had drawn in the middle for them to aim at. Amelia was elated, too, and wasn't too reserved to keep from whooping and jumping up and down a couple of times.

"All right, ladies, do that a few more times, then we'll back up about ten paces."

All three enjoyed themselves as they identified weaknesses in technique and accuracy and made adjustments. They were so involved, they were startled when they heard a voice from behind them.

"Don't shoot, I come in peace," Gann called out, stopping a reasonable distance away and dismounting his horse.

"You're just in time for some fun," Lacy said.

"I hoped I'd be just in time for supper," he responded, and his dimples showed themselves again.

"You're in time for that, too. I made a buttermilk pie today for dessert."

"I'll have that; you all can have the rest of the food."

That brought a few more chuckles before they settled back into target practice. Lacy noticed they seemed to divide into two groups with Gann helping Amelia much more than he commented on how well she was doing.

Later, as the ladies put dinner on the table, Gann asked Emmett if there were any updates on the situation in Laramie.

"I got a wire today with some news, but now we have even more questions," he answered as they sat down to eat. "Deacon and Tillie will be back in town day after tomorrow, and we plan to meet them when they arrive and get more details."

"Oh, Mother, if you don't come with us, we'll be happy to mail your letters for you."

"I think I'll stay here again, so thank you for offering to do that."

"If you want the letters to go out immediately, I'll be happy to take you to town tomorrow," Gann said. "Besides, I can always find a few things at the mercantile I just have to have. We can look around and maybe stop for coffee at Mary's before coming back."

"That would be wonderful, Gann. You really don't mind?"

"Of course not. It'll be my pleasure. Maybe when we get back, I can show you how to shoot a rifle since you're so good with your pistol. I think you'll like a rifle. They're mighty powerful."

"That sounds good. I can practice some more with the Colt, too."

"Good idea. Wild Bill Hickok was said to have been partial to Colts. He had a Navy and a Dragoon, I believe."

"Wild Bill must have been a pretty popular item around here. You and Emmett both mentioned him."

Gann grinned and Lacy suddenly understood what her mother might see in him. "Not really, it's just that most of our lives, rumors and stories and articles about Hickok came up all the time. And I'm pretty sure you can't believe half of them."

Lacy laughed. "If we keep practicing, we'll get so good you'll start hearing rumors and stories about us, won't they, Mother?"

Gann chimed in again. "I would like to see you both get competent and confident shooting. I don't know if Emmett mentioned it, but did he tell you the cardinal rule around here? If you need help or run into any kind of problem, fire three shots in succession. We'll stop whatever we're doing and come to help. It's the same plan several people in town use, including the sheriff."

"That was one of the first things he told us," Amelia said.

"Good. I just want to make sure," Gann said.

THAT NIGHT as they were getting ready for bed, Emmett noticed Lacy's demeanor. "Something's bothering you, darlin', I can tell. Tell me what it is."

"Nothing really, I don't think. Well, maybe. I think Amelia likes Gann."

"Of course, she does. He's a likeable man."

"Emmett, I mean romantically."

"Oh. Is that a bad thing? They might do well together. Come to think of it, we have been seeing a lot of him over here. When she first came out here, I wondered about how they might get together, but then I dismissed it."

"Maybe they would be good together as a couple. They get along well. But don't you think it's too soon after Father's death for her to be getting romantic?"

Emmett looked at her and smiled reassuringly. "No, I don't think so. From what you tell me and what Amelia's said, your mother and father had a close, happy relationship. Even after his health changed things, they were still best friends, still comforting companions. I imagine your mother feels the loss of that relationship very sharply. She has us, but it's not the same thing. Whether she realizes she's doing it or not, she's probably searching for something to fill that void in her life. She misses what she had with your father. And I remember him telling her to move on and find another best friend. You heard it, too. If she has his blessing, it's not up to us to judge."

She smiled. "Yes, I remember it, too. You're right. I do want to see her happily married again."

"Good. So if it happens, be happy for them."

"I will."

They were quiet for several minutes as they climbed into bed, and Emmett burst out laughing. "If they do get married, I'll start calling him Uncle Dad."

Lacy cackled. "And Aunt Mother! Just think, if they have a baby, I'll be both a sibling and a cousin to him."

He laughed more. "And if we have one, he'll be both Gann's grandson and his great-nephew. Oh, and ours will be their baby's nephew and cousin. Wait, is that right? I'm getting confused."

"First cousin once removed," Lacy corrected with a laugh, then she got quiet. "Emmett?"

"Hmm?" he said as he pulled her closer and guided her head to his shoulder so his arm would go around her.

"That might be sooner than you think."

He looked down at her and saw her softened expression and her hand on her tummy.

"You mean?" He put his hand on her tummy, too.

"I'm pretty sure. Probably in about seven months."

Emmett pulled her to him and smothered her with kisses in between the smiles and chuckles and words telling her how happy he was. That led to other things, and soon the words of happiness turned into words of passionate heat.

Later, Lacy asked Emmett not to tell anyone just yet. She wanted it to be their sweet secret for a few days first. He agreed.

THIRTEEN

Gann arrived earlier than they had arranged for the trip into town.

"I thought we might as well have lunch at Mary's, then we can shop. I hope you don't mind that I changed plans without asking you."

"I don't mind at all," Amelia said. "It sounds delightful. Let me go get my letters."

Emmett and Lacy exchanged quick looks and his told her he now understood what she'd mentioned the night before.

They stood on the porch waving goodbye and telling Gann and Amelia to have a nice time. As they watched them drive away in the wagon, Emmett yelled out, "Gann, bring back some butter. We're about out."

Gann raised his arm in acknowledgement and called out, "Will do," but he didn't turn around to look at them. A moment or two later, the wagon was out of sight, having rounded the curve and started down one of the straight stretches of the road.

Lacy started to walk back inside the house, but Emmett stopped her, telling her to stay outside with him. He grabbed her and kissed her almost roughly, but not quite. His hands roamed over her backside before one came between them to fondle her breasts. She responded by purring and pushing herself into him so hard, he had to move one foot to steady himself.

"Oh, Em, I don't know what it is, but the last couple of weeks, it seems like I can't get enough of you."

Emmett pulled back away to look at her and began to unbutton her bodice. His fingers fumbled and he finally said, "Oh, hell, I'll buy you new clothes," as he ripped hers off her body.

Her body reacted to his animal passion with warmth and a dewy wetness, but she still had a hesitation. "Emmett! Out here? It's daylight."

"Nobody's around. I've been waiting for your mother to be gone so we can try out this swing."

"Oh..." she said as he shucked the rest of his clothes, sat down on the swing, and beckoned to her with a curled finger and a lascivious look.

They had an awkward moment as they figured how to get her placed astride him with her legs going through the open area of the swing between the seat and the back. As Emmett lifted her down onto him, Lacy expressed her appreciation—and her awe—that he was so hard, she had to peel his length away from his belly to guide it inside her. Her eyes held his as she lowered and it filled her, then she had to close her eyes as her breath quickened. They both moaned with the intensity of that intimate contact.

He put his arms around her and kissed her as he slowly began to propel the swing with his feet. Lacy relished the feel of him inside her, but she lamented that her feet didn't reach the porch floor and she had no way to instigate movements or thrusts.

After a few gentle swings, he asked her how it felt.

"Well, it feels pleasant—"

He cut her off. "Pleasant? *Pleasant?* Lacy, that's how you described afternoon tea with the Ladies' Aid Society. I'm hoping for more than pleasant here." He gave her a rueful grin as he shook his head and propelled the swing faster.

"Well, can you thrust up into me?"

He tried, but with their positions and the fact that he couldn't keep his feet on the floorboards for continued leverage, his drives weren't rhythmic or terribly powerful. He put his fingers on her nub and began the motions he knew she liked best.

"Does this help?" he asked, but she only moaned and made a few other noises that weren't quite words.

He watched her reactions to his movements, watched her bring her own hands up to her breasts to caress and tweak her nipples. It nearly drove him to his own completion. He stopped the swing, held on to her and stood, taking care that her legs came safely through the open area of the swing. As soon as she was free of it, he turned her around and bent her over the porch rail. One hand was on her back, holding her down, and the other nudged her legs apart, then he entered her again. He pounded her hard with driving, forceful lunges that made her grunt involuntarily. Her breasts swung wildly, not really back and forth, but with a rounded motion. Emmett watched them and thought they might have swollen some already. He was about to reach down to play with one of them when he heard Lacy's build-up sounds. He pounded her even harder and, somehow, even faster, as the sweat dripped off his face and ran down his chest. They both shuddered their release at the same time.

Emmett put a hand on either side of her on the porch rail and leaned on it for support while he caught his breath again.

While her breath and heartbeat hadn't quite returned to

normal, Lacy went ahead and commented, "So, porch swing, no; porch rail, resounding yes."

Emmett laughed. *"Pleasant*, my ass."

GANN AND AMELIA enjoyed their ride into town. Gann proved to be charming, with a quick wit that held a hint of sarcasm. Amelia held up her side of the conversation with some comebacks that had Gann laughing out loud.

"Oh, up ahead's that bend in the road that might be a good spot to build a house. Tell me where you'd build if it were yours," Amelia asked.

"All right," he answered. "It might take us a little longer to get it built than we first thought. With the new church building project taking shape, we both will likely have to put in a good deal of time with it."

"That's fine. I wouldn't want to interfere with the Lord's work," she said with a smile. "Besides, we have no time frame at all, no deadlines for me. My only consideration is giving the newlyweds privacy in their own home, but they don't act eager for me to move out." She laughed again. "At least to my face."

Gann glanced at her with a grin that flashed his dimples and made her melt. Or it might have been his seductive eyes, she wasn't sure.

"I think newlyweds will find that kind of privacy no matter the obstacle. I believe they're enjoying your company. I am."

Despite her quick wit and sharp thinking, Amelia couldn't come up with a response that said what she thought without it sounding too forward. She grinned at him and hoped that said enough.

When they came to the bend, Gann pointed out where he'd build if he were going to live there. He pointed out where he'd dig the well, where he'd put the barn, the chicken coop, a vegetable patch and maybe even a workshop for his wood-building hobby. As he described it all and pointed at the locations, Amelia was reminded that she had so many decisions to make, not only about the house, but regarding her future, too. What *did* she want?

Their easy and companionable conversation continued throughout their outing. They went first to the restaurant, then they went straight to the stagecoach office to drop off her letters. The mail service was convenient in town; letters could be dropped off at either the mercantile, which was what most people used, or at the stagecoach office since ultimately, that's where mail either arrived by stage or left by stage. Every day, Clint Keller, who owned the mercantile, took the posted items over to the stage office before the stage arrived, and every day when the stage left, the stationmaster took the mail that had arrived over to the mercantile, where Clint would sort it in cubbies.

The two strolled down the street to the telegraph office to see if either Gann or Emmett had received wires. Neither had.

They stopped just for a few minutes at the dressmaker's shop, where Amelia admired a few dresses and accessories but didn't purchase anything. Gann surprised her by offering to buy them for her, but she politely refused. Purchasing clothing for someone seemed like such an intimate gesture and her feelings were conflicted.

They had saved the mercantile as the last stop in town since they had to take butter home and might likely pick up other perishables. While there, they picked up a few other things and headed home. Conversation turned to target practice and he told her about his rifle, and by the time they arrived at Emmett's house, Amelia was eager to shoot again.

Emmett and Lacy had recovered and cleaned themselves

and were enjoying a cup of coffee at the kitchen table when the other couple came in. Gann handed Emmett the butter and didn't wait for him to say *thank you* before he said, "You're welcome."

"Mother, how was your trip to town?"

Amelia answered from across the room where she was picking up her pistol. "We had a most pleasant time."

Emmett and Lacy exchanged surreptitious looks and managed not to snicker at the use of the word *pleasant* before Lacy responded, "Good, I'm glad."

"We're about to go outside for some target practice and I'm going to show Amelia how to shoot a rifle. You two should come on out and shoot with us." Gann was already ushering Amelia out the door as he spoke, and he didn't wait for a response.

Emmett and Lacy chuckled once they were alone.

When they were outside and out of earshot, Amelia chuckled, too. "You were right about newlyweds overcoming obstacles. That was a different dress from the one she was wearing when we left."

THE NEXT MORNING held some excitement for the young couple, since they planned to meet Deacon and Tillie Snow and find out the rest of the story of what had happened in Laramie. They were both eager to hear what had transpired.

"Mother, why don't you go with us? You're welcome to, you know."

"No, but thank you for the invitation. I believe I'll stay here again and see what kind of trouble I can get into on my own. I'm not sure I'm in the mood to hear all about Laramie goings-on right now. You can fill me in when you get home."

"All right, then, we'll see you when we get back later this afternoon," Lacy said as she kissed her mother's cheek.

Amelia walked them outside and waved goodbye from the porch until their buggy was out of sight. She sat down on the porch swing, just enjoying the solitude and scenery for a few minutes. Thinking that flower beds would be attractive along the front of the porch, she made a mental note to ask Emmett if he minded if they put some in. She smiled inwardly, knowing he wouldn't mind at all. But it would be a nice gesture to ask. She said a quick prayer to thank God for sending Emmett for Lacy. That had been a blessing for all of them.

Amelia stood and stepped down the porch to walk around the yard. She noted another place or two where a flower bed would be ideal. As she walked around the house, she thought that since the chicken coop was patterned after a tiny version of the house, it should have tiny flower beds in front of it, too. The idea made her laugh out loud and she knew they had to do it. Gann would love it.

Gann? Where did that come from?

She walked around the coop, almost mesmerized by the movements of the chickens as they pecked at the ground. Then she left the chickens and walked over to the clothesline, running her hands along the wiry cording for a few feet before she walked on farther back toward the river. She loved the water, at least she loved watching it. It gave her a peaceful feeling to see the gentle flow, and it delighted her when a fish surfaced. She smiled at the memory of George and the pastor going fishing and George catching nothing. She smiled even bigger when she realized the memory of George no longer hurt her heart.

She walked on with a fresh, renewed spirit, following the river. When she realized she wasn't in the yard any longer, a small, guilty panic came over her. She looked back toward the house and could still see it, but barely. Amelia decided she was still close enough, and besides, she didn't want to walk all the way back to get her pistol.

The water called to her and she walked, letting it guide her. The trail, the one that led to Gann's house, was roughly parallel to the water, sometimes close to it, sometimes farther away. As she chose her steps to stay near the water, she saw why the trail was crooked in some places. There were stands of trees or boulders or other obstacles in the way. Amelia thought it made for a picturesque setting and wondered why she hadn't noticed it before when Emmett had taken them to Gann's house.

She heard the rapids before she saw them and hurried to reach them. Amelia stopped to admire the rocky edge that led down to the turbulent water. She marveled at the foamy white-caps that formed where the water was forced over rocks and boulders. The power of nature was amazing to her, and yet these rapids weren't nearly as big as some she'd heard of. How lovely that running water would feel over her feet, she thought.

Amelia knew she had probably gone much too far to suit Emmett, especially without a gun handy, and she decided to turn back and go home.

No, I'm going to feel that water on my feet first, then I'll head back.

She took off her shoes and was glad she hadn't put on stockings that morning. She made her way carefully across the grassy dirt, then onto the big rocks at the water's edge. When she realized the wet rocks nearest the river were slippery, she slowed and carefully chose her steps. She spied the rock she wanted to sit on; it would be perfect for dangling her feet in the water. As she made her way to it and bent to sit, she lost her balance and fell forward into the currents.

EMMETT AND LACY again enjoyed their ride into town alone, but this time they talked about what might have happened in Laramie almost as much as they flirted and talked about intimate things.

Tillie Snow was surprised to find them waiting at the stage-coach office, but Deacon wasn't. He had an inkling Emmett would be too curious to wait for information. The Snows accepted their invitation to lunch, and they made their way over there.

"Aren't you going to give us any hints?" Emmett asked on the way.

"Well, Lacy, I can tell you that you are no longer under suspicion in any way. It never would have amounted to anything, of course, but Faust is no longer accusing you. Indeed, he's the one who finally admitted you had nothing to do with the murders."

Lacy let out a big sigh of relief. "I can't wait to hear those details."

Deacon laughed. "You'll have to wait until Mary's taken our order, then I'll tell you more than you can imagine."

They settled in at the table and Mary took their orders. As they watched her walk away, Deacon said, "I hardly know where to begin. I will say, though, that once they brought in the US Marshal, things fell into place pretty quickly."

"About that, how did you get them to call the Marshals?" Emmett asked.

"I tried to talk to the deputy about my own findings, and he wouldn't hear anything I had to say."

"It's true," Tillie added, "he just argued back with things that were ridiculous. It was clear to us that Deputy Faust had lost reason. Sometimes he looked like a cornered rat, looking around for a way to escape."

Deacon continued. "Sheriff Faust, the father, came into the

office while we were trying to get the deputy to at least listen to what we had to say. I don't think he had any idea his son was in such a bad mental state. He backed his son up, but we could tell he was skeptical of some of the things Faust was saying."

"Like what?"

"Like continuing to blame Lacy. And other things, too, but it really didn't matter at that point. Tillie and I went to see the judge and laid out all our evidence and explained Faust's position. Judge Barrett wasn't too surprised; I don't think he thought much of Faust. Anyway, he called in the Marshals Service and wrote up some kind of order removing Faust from the case. He turned over jurisdiction to the marshal. When Justin Turner, the marshal, arrived, we sat down with him and went over everything. I've known Justin for years and he's a good man."

Mary brought out more drinks and bowls of bread and butter and set them on the table.

"Justin got to business immediately. When he found out Alan had been hanged out at his relative's property, he decided to go check Alan's place in town. Alan had rented a small house on the edge of the seedier section of town. Justin found arsenic. Granted, you'll find it in plenty of other houses, too, to kill vermin and such, but you don't usually find it in a shaving kit. That made it handy to have on hand when he went to stay at the Nixon's home overnight."

"So Alan killed Carl's parents?" Lacy asked.

"Yes. Slowly and agonizingly. He apparently wanted to hasten any inheritance. The doctor was keeping them out with laudanum a good bit of the time, as much as he dared, to spare them pain. That's how Carl's killers were able to shoot a gun and not wake them."

"I hadn't even thought of that," Lacy said. "Wait, killers? Plural?"

Deacon smiled ruefully. "It might be better if I go back to

the beginning. As you both know, the deputy had his sights set on Lacy. And when you entered the picture, Emmett, someone who had dealt him a humiliating blow in the past, his desire to get what he thought of as rightful vengeance intensified against both of you. First, he wanted to prevent your marriage to Carl, Lacy. He decided to go over to Carl's house the morning of the wedding and try to blackmail Carl into not going through with it. He planned to tell people that Carl and Alan were sodomites. I never did find out how he knew, but we speculate that Deputy Faust may have had the same leanings. That may help explain why he tried outwardly to present such a manly appearance, why he was so rough, especially with women."

Mary brought out their main courses, so he paused in his narrative.

"All right, now, continue," Emmett said as he picked up his fork.

"So the deputy went to Carl's house, only to find that Carl had already been shot. But he wasn't dead. He was able to speak and told Faust that Alan had shot him earlier and left him for dead. He begged Faust to fetch you so he could explain things to you directly, but he refused. He began to speculate that he could have both you and Carl out of the way if he pinned it on you. He would say that you found out about Alan and shot him. Then he'd only have Alan to kill and his revenge would be complete. At that point, Emmett, you hadn't come into the picture."

Emmett shook his head. "That's quite a tenuous plan."

"Apparently not for Faust," Tillie said.

"Anyway," Deacon went on, "Faust shot Carl and this time, the bullet killed him. He decided to leave and wait for someone to find him. It didn't take long. Gerald came to pick up Carl and take him to the wedding. When he found him dead, he remembered seeing the deputy a couple of streets over, and hurried to get him. Faust played his part perfectly and went with Gerald to inform you of Carl's death."

Deacon paused to take a few bites of his meatloaf and potatoes. Emmett and Lacy reflected on what they'd heard so far.

"So then Faust tracked Alan down to his relative's cabin and went to kill him. He decided to find another way to kill him so it would be easier to pin it on someone else, presumably Lacy's accomplice. Or better yet, make it look like a suicide. Alan was expecting to be chased down and arrested since he thought he'd killed Carl. He was relieved to hear that he hadn't killed him, but terrified when the deputy immediately told him that he was going to kill him so he couldn't tell anyone that he, the deputy, had killed Carl. Alan lunged at him, but Faust was a wiry and quick little guy, and he landed a good blow with his fist that knocked Alan out. With him out, it was easy for the deputy to hang him. The guy never knew what happened to him."

"I guess that only leaves me on his hit list. Maybe Lacy, unless he thinks he can have her," Emmett said.

"No need to worry about that. Deputy Faust has already met his maker," Deacon said with his mouth still chewing a small bite.

"How the hell did that happen?" Emmett asked.

"When Justin went out to the place where Alan was hanged, he realized that it had to be murder, too. There was nothing for him to stand on that he could kick away. No place for him to put a noose around his neck and jump or fall to his hanging death. Someone else had to have hanged him. Justin knew it had to be Faust. I went with him to the sheriff's office to arrest Faust, and that's when he finally saw that he was cornered. He confessed everything, including his hatred for you, Emmett. Faust's gun belt hung on a hook on the wall. When Justin approached to handcuff him, Faust jumped to grab his pistol. He was drawing up his arm to take a shot when the sheriff stopped him. With a bullet. Shot his own son."

"Oh, my," Lacy said.

"It was very hard on him. When I talked to him last, he was planning to move away soon. He couldn't get past the guilt for having believed his son for so long that he allowed justice to be denied. I think he's an honest man torn between family and his duty by the law."

"I surely do appreciate your work on this, Deacon, and clearing my wife's name." He chuckled. "I imagine the people of Laramie are grateful, too, for being rid of the deputy."

"I still feel so bad for Carl and his parents. They really were nice people," Lacy said. "Even Alan was nice to me. I still find it hard to believe he killed Carl's parents."

"I suspect he wanted to pin it on Gerald, so Carl would get the inheritance. I've no way of knowing, but it makes sense. Gerald was enough of a bad boy for that to be believable."

Lacy agreed.

"Do you have a bill for me?" Emmett asked.

"I'll put it together soon."

"All right, perfect. I know you two must be tired from the trip. Again, we sure thank you for all your work."

GANN'S HORSE ambled down the trail; he only occasionally coaxed him into a faster pace for a few minutes.

Gann knew Amelia was by herself for a bit today while Emmett and Lacy went to talk to Deacon. No matter how he tried, he couldn't keep himself away. Besides, maybe she would think it would be nice to have his company so she wouldn't be alone.

He was lost in thoughts of Amelia when he heard a faint

voice calling for help. He jumped to attention and focused on his hearing as he hollered, "Call out again!"

He heard it and spurred his horse into action, headed for the sound. He jumped down when he arrived and saw the back of a head and arms reaching out of the water, holding on to exposed tree roots.

"I'm coming, I'm here, just hold on for a few more seconds," he said. He reached her in no time and stepped into the water up to his thighs to pick her up. He was so shocked, he nearly dropped her when he realized who it was.

"Amelia! What happened?"

But she was too weak to respond just yet. Her breathing was shallow and fast and all she could manage to say was, "Gann."

"I've got you, just be still," he said as he looked around and found a fairly smooth boulder to sit on as he held her.

He held her cradled in his arms, his emotions running wild inside him. *How the hell did she get in the water? Why was she out alone? Why hadn't she fired three shots for help? Where was she headed, to my house? Will she be all right?* His hold on her varied by the dominant emotion at that moment.

Finally, her breath returned to nearly normal and she found words. "Thank Heaven you came by, Gann. I thought for sure I was going to die here."

"I'd never let that happen." His hold became tighter. "I could have lost you." That thought cinched it. He lifted her enough to turn her over his knee and started swatting. "You should know better than to let yourself get into a situation like that. Why didn't you fire three shots like we told you?"

"I didn't bring my gun," she almost shouted, as though she were saying the words *I'll be good, I'll bring it next time.*

The admission that she didn't have her gun with her made

him more determined to make an impression on her backside. "Damn fool woman," he mumbled.

"I'm sorry!" she managed to say between snuffles.

"And another thing," he said, "no more talk about building a new house. You'll live in my house, you understand? You're going to marry me. Me, dammit. You're going to marry me!"

"Yes, yes, I'll marry you!" her little voice answered back from somewhere near the ground.

He stopped and pulled her up and back onto his lap, inside his arms, his face next to hers, just holding her. "You're going to marry me, you hear? Amelia, I could have lost you."

With that, he pulled his head back a little and cradled her head in his hands. The kiss started gently then became almost desperate, and they both thought it matched all the emotions they were both going through.

When that kiss was over, he held her a few moments more. "I'd better get you home and out of these wet clothes. We're both soaking wet now."

On the way, she told him how it happened that she fell in. He just shook his head. "Woman, I've a mind to spank you again for ignoring the natural fact that wet rocks are slick."

She sighed and leaned back against him. "Would you at least wait until I'm feeling better?"

If she'd turned to look at him, she'd have seen a grin on his face.

"I imagine it can wait. When we get there, you go run a tub of hot water. I'll go find some of Emmett's britches to wear, then I'll fix a pot of tea. I think I'll lace yours with brandy."

"That sure sounds good to me."

EMMETT AND LACY came home to the sight of Amelia's wet clothes draped over the porch rails. Gann's wet britches were spread out over the swing and his socks were over an armrest. His boots were upside down on a boot-drying rack he had made and given to Emmett a few years ago.

"What the hell's been going on here?" Emmett asked under his breath, knowing Lacy wanted to know the same thing.

He didn't bother to put away the horses and buggy just yet. They went inside to find Gann relaxing in an overstuffed chair, a cup of tea in his hand.

"Where's Mother?" Lacy asked.

"In the bath," Gann answered. "You might want to go attend to her."

Lacy went to her mother. Emmett sat down on the couch across from Gann.

"All right, spill. What happened?"

"Your mother-in-law fell in the rapids and I happened to come along just in time to find her about to pass out. She'd managed to grab onto some roots on the bank of the calm pool."

"Oh, Lord, is she all right?"

"Pretty battered and she'll be badly bruised, but she'll be fine."

"What was she doing?"

"Taking a walk." Gann looked up at Emmett. "Without her pistol."

Emmett's expression changed to one of grave concern. "We both told her to always take a gun if she goes that far. I mean, both of us told them that."

Gann nodded in agreement.

Emmett leaned forward, his sense of responsibility coming to the fore. "Gann? Do you think I'm going to have to take my own mother-in-law in hand? I never expected this to come up."

"No need to. I already took care of it," Gann said.

Emmett looked up in surprise. "What do you mean? Did you..."

"I did; I definitely did. I also told her she's going to marry me, and she agreed."

Emmett looked dumbfounded for a moment while that soaked in. "Well, hell," he said as he jumped up. "We need to drink a toast to that."

"I believe I could use some whiskey right now," Gann agreed.

EPILOGUE

Lacy received the brand new Singer sewing machine Emmett ordered, and after making herself some maternity clothes and some gowns for the baby, she got back into her artistic roots. Her pieces hung in their home and in Gann and Amelia's, and soon people who saw her fabric portraits were begging her to make wall hangings for them.

It turned out that Gann and Amelia were the first couple married in the new church. She didn't want to move into his house until it had hot running water, and since a good bit of his time was taken up overseeing the building of the church, it took some time to finish both projects. It was the one firm contingency she set on the wedding date and Gann let her get away with it.

Harriet was so pleased to see her friend Gann married that she gave them a paddle for a wedding gift, too. Gann appreciated the thoughtful gesture. Amelia, not so much. She appreciated his quiet authority, just not the paddle. But it was noteworthy that she never again ventured far from the house without her pistol handy.

Emmett Burke, Jr. was born, weighing in at nearly eight

pounds. He had a happy disposition and was the handsome image of his father. Lacy joked that she expected to have to turn the girls away when he became older. He was such a blessing to them that a year and a half later when they learned the boy would become an older brother, they had a big family celebration. It was a double celebration because Amelia, too, was expecting.

Gerald Nixon inherited his parents' home, business, and bank account. He tried to live in the house but couldn't. He couldn't sleep, knowing his brother and parents had died there. It wasn't exactly ghosts he saw or heard, but he knew it was a sense that they were still there. He sold the properties, cleared out the bank account, settled his gambling debts and moved. He never told anyone where.

Laramie was a faded memory. Sheriff Faust resigned and moved away, and nobody knew where he went, either. Neither Amelia nor Lacy ever wanted to go back to visit, and that suited Emmett and Gann just fine.

The End

NORA NOLAN

Nora Nolan is one of my pen names. It's nice to meet you! I love to read all kinds of books. All kinds! So far, though, I've only written one basic type. They usually have fairly normal, sexy, fun relationships between the main characters, infused with a little wicked kink. So if you like age play, strong D/s lifestyles, or women in chains who beg to be caned, you might want to look for other authors. I'm not there yet.

My newest joy is sitting at the keyboard, letting the characters in my head write their stories. They often lead me in directions that surprise me. I never know when I start out what direction they'll take or where they'll end up.

I live in the southern central part of the US. My happier days find me with our family, or spending time with my wonderful alpha husband.

Email Nora directly at NoraNolan.books@gmail.com
Website: https://www.noranolanbooks.com

Don't miss these exciting titles by Nora Nolan and Blushing Books!

Operation Big Rock Brides (*Historical Western*)
Two Brides for Big Rock
Opal from Omaha
Ruby from Rawlins
Lacy from Laramie

BLUSHING BOOKS

Blushing Books is the oldest eBook publisher on the web. We've been running websites that publish steamy romance and erotica since 1999, and we have been selling eBooks since 2003. We have free and promotional offerings that change weekly, so please do visit us at http://www.blushingbooks.com/free.

BLUSHING BOOKS NEWSLETTER

Please join the Blushing Books newsletter
to receive updates & special promotional offers.
You can also join by using your mobile phone:
Just text BLUSHING to 22828.

Every month, one new sign up via text messaging will
receive a $25.00 Amazon gift card so sign up today!

www.ingramcontent.com/pod-product-compliance
Lightning Source LLC
Chambersburg PA
CBHW060937180626
46817CB00004B/1593